Night Sounds
and Other Stories

Karen Gettert Shoemaker's fiction, nonfiction, and poetry have appeared in numerous literary journals, trade magazines, anthologies, and newspapers. A native of Nebraska, she holds a Master's Degree and a Ph.D. in Creative Writing from the University of Nebraska-Lincoln. She has received the Vreeland Award for Fiction from UN-L and a Nebraska Press Association Award. She taught writing and literature classes at UN-L for nine years and currently conducts writing workshops with students from kindergarten to adult. She and her husband have two children. This is her first book.

NIGHT SOUNDS
AND OTHER STORIES

KAREN GETTERT SHOEMAKER

DUFOUR EDITIONS

First published in the United States of America, 2002
by Dufour Editions Inc., Chester Springs, Pennsylvania 19425

Cover photograph by Randy Barger.
Graphic design, front cover by Reynold Peterson

"Witness" reprinted by permission
of the author, Pam Herbert Barger.

ISBN 0-8023-1337-X

Library of Congress Cataloging-in-Publication Data

Shoemaker, Karen Gettert, 1957-
   Night sounds and other stories / Karen Gettert Shoemaker.
      p. cm.
   ISBN 0-8023-1337-X
   1. Middle West--Social life and customs--Fiction. I. Title.

PS3619.H64 N54 2002
813'.6--dc21
                                                    2001058489

Printed and bound in the United States of America

To Dave, Ryan, and Raina

Some of the stories in this collection first appeared (some in different form) in the following publications: "Seams" in *South Dakota Review;* "Dyanna's Face Reflected in Glass" in *Laurus;* "Charley and Evelyn's Party" in *Foliage;* "A Funny Story" in *Kalliope;* "Glossolalia" in *West Wind Review;* "Night Sounds" in *Heartlands Today;* "Orphans" in *Credo;* "Playing Horses" in *Prairie Schooner;* "Scar" in *The Nebraska Review.*

Contents

Do not be misled by
that which feels true; these
stories are works of fiction.

PLAYING HORSES

The first time Bobbi came back for a visit, my mother warned me she might have outgrown me. "She might have matured faster than you did," were her exact words. I was helping her hang the wash on the line that stretched across the back yard when she told me this. As always, I was in charge of clothespins. I straddled a little red wagon and scooched along behind her, imagining the wagon a prairie schooner and the wet clothes around me canyon walls. I didn't answer her. I just handed her another clothespin and thought about Bobbi's visit.

In her latest letter she had told me she was going to bring pictures of the horses in the field across from her house.

"I wake up every morning and first thing I do is look out and see them in the field. I always pretend that the palomino is mine and the big black one is yours because I know how much you like black horses," she had written. She didn't sound any different than when she left. Even though my Mom said she probably was a whole lot more grown up than I was I went on planning her visit as if she were still my best friend. Just as she had been when she moved away.

The neighborhood where Bobbi and I had been friends

was full of kids but few friends. My family lived in a rundown house with a big yard that wrapped around the last house on the block like the cookie that's left after the bite. On one side we looked toward a trailer court, on the other toward rentals in varying degrees of disrepair. Both of those views were superior to what adjoined us on the north. On that side, across a narrow alley, was our little town's little slum. Nine or ten houses on one block that we all called, for reasons that still escape me, "Goat Alley." We were better than anybody on that street, and on the other streets most people moved in and out so fast we hardly had time to get to know them.

Only three families stayed in our neighborhood for any length of time and we had something like sixteen or seventeen kids between us. The neighborhood felt full and we all felt we belonged to something bigger than ourselves. We weren't much. We didn't love each other intensely or even like each other all that much all the time. But we were familiar to one another and that seemed to count for something. When the chill wind of winter blew into town we knew we could count on one another to show up next summer for the next baseball season. We could trust one another to remember who hit a home run and who had to climb over Old Man Ogden's fence to retrieve the lucky ball.

On the other hand, rental people came and went in no discernible pattern, and you couldn't be sure they would be there next week much less next season, so what was the point of them? You might play hide and seek with them some evening, or let them in on neighborhood games just to even up sides when necessary, but if push came to shove, it was us against them. We were a team and no rental kid was going to get in on that solid front. We even made up a rule just so they would know their place. We said, loudly and often, that you couldn't be a real neighbor until you had lived in your house for five years.

Okay, so we weren't much. We knew that. There's an ugliness that comes with that kind of knowing. It wasn't that we had a leader we followed into trouble, it was that we didn't and so we sometimes followed a base instinct to be better than something. If it hadn't been rental kids it would have been something else. Each other maybe. Probably.

All our parents worked during the day. In the early days of the neighborhood there may have been some kind of day care arrangements, but by the time I came along the authority figure in most households was an older brother or sister. If we were alive at the end of the day they had lived up to their responsibility.

Once, on one of those long unsupervised days, my brother and one of neighbor boys decided they didn't want us girls playing in the same yard they were in. They told us to "Get out or die."

Mary and Lucy yelled a few names at them, used words they shouldn't have even known, but they did it over their shoulders on their way to another yard. I don't know if I was being stupid that day or rebellious or what, but I said no, I wasn't going anywhere. We were there first.

"Anyway, it's my yard and you can't make me leave," I said. I sat down on the grass to prove my point.

The boys just looked at each other and laughed. They didn't say anything to each other. They just knew what to do.

My brother grabbed one ankle and the neighbor boy grabbed the other.

"You're gonna wish you left when you had the chance," one of them said. Then they took off running.

I wasn't much more than nine at the time and my little girl body wasn't much weight for two teenage boys. They ran through the garden where last year's cornstalks stuck up from the ground like spikes. They didn't slow down until they got to the gravel driveway and then only because they were laughing so hard they couldn't run anymore. I screamed the whole time and that seemed to make it funnier.

When I rolled over to stand up the sight of my bloody back scared them into silence.

"Oh shit, we're dead," one of them said finally and then the neighbor boy took off as if there was someplace to hide in this neighborhood.

My brother knew there was no where to go and at first he just stood there staring at me, saying, "Oh shit oh shit oh shit oh shit."

I know it was fear of the punishment in store for him that made him help me into the house, but I also know there was remorse, kindness even, in his touch when he washed my back, carefully wiping away the mud, cleaning the cuts with peroxide. He kept saying, "I'm sorry. I'm sorry." And I kept crying. "It hurts. It hurts."

Maybe I should have forgiven him. He looked so sorry standing there with that bloody wash cloth in his hand and his touch on my back was so soft it felt like love. But when I turned around and gingerly pulled my shirt down he said, "Don't tell Dad." Just because it feels like love doesn't mean it is.

I did tell Dad, and when my brother got the belt that night I plugged my ears and didn't cry. My Dad couldn't do anything about the neighbor boy, but the boy didn't know that. He stayed away from our house for a month after that.

As I said, we weren't much, and we knew it. But we weren't rental kids either, so we had something to stand on. Looking back at all this, at the run-down state of all our houses and the little secrets we hid behind closed doors, it is downright shocking that we had the gall to affect snobbishness.

But affect it we did, and that's the world Bobbi dropped into when her Mom and Dad dropped their double wide in the corner of what was supposed to be our baseball field. No one in the neighborhood was going to ever forgive the Kellers for messing up a perfectly good baseball field, and until that summer I didn't know I could do anything different than what the neighborhood did. For three whole weeks after they moved in, Mary, Lucy, and I made a point of not playing with Bobbi. We played right in front of her house just so she would know we weren't playing with her. We would take sticks out of her yard to draw hopscotch squares in the dirt road in front of her house. When suppertime came we threw our stones into her yard like so much trash. I can still see her small white face peering out the window at us. Watching while we pretended she didn't exist.

It would be easy to paint Bobbi as some kind of savior in this scene, some kind of second – better – part of me, but that wouldn't be completely honest. She was just a girl my age that lived near me for a while. In the way of proximity we became friends, in the way of young girls we became Best Friends.

I'm not sure where Mary and Lucy were that day I first talked to Bobbi. I just remember that I was alone and I was doing what I always did when no one was around – I was pretending to be a wild horse.

After all these years I can still recall how real my imagination made this game. Words just aren't enough to explain it and saying it now makes me laugh, but back then it was serious business. Our yard, the biggest in the neighborhood and with the most trees, was big enough to hold a tropical island, a mountain range, and high plains so wide you couldn't walk from one side to the other in a day's time. I didn't need Mary or Lucy. I didn't need anybody. I was a wild stallion, the fastest, strongest, wildest, most beautiful wild stallion that ever walked the earth. As a little girl I was timid and clumsy, but when I became a horse I became everything I ever knew about power and freedom.

Sometimes even now, when the late afternoon light is slanting just so across green space or through trees I can remember just exactly what it felt like to take on that magic. I can close my eyes, breathe deeply and feel my velvety nostrils flare, picking up the scent of danger, freedom.

That day, alone in my yard, in the small part between the house on the corner and the alley, I was running from wolves when suddenly I saw Bobbi across the street. She was leaping across fallen trees and dodging branches. She stopped and at first I thought she was looking at me, but then I realized she didn't see anything that was around her. She tossed her hair back and lifted her nose to the wind. I knew that movement like I knew the beating of my own heart. She was pretending to be a horse! I swear my ears pricked up, flickered in an attempt to hear her. Somehow or another I found myself across the street in her yard, and then we were in mine. We didn't talk that first day. Instead, we just raced and jumped and dodged, not needing to explain what we were running from or jumping over or dodging around. Like horses, we just knew. Isn't that what friendship is supposed to be?

That's what I thought, and more importantly, I believed it could stay that way. When Bobbi's anxiously awaited visit came I was standing on the porch waiting. As soon as I saw them pull up I raced out to the car to meet her. My mom frowned at my obviously childish behavior when I jumped off the porch, but I went right ahead and galloped toward the car. For her part, the allegedly more mature Bobbi came out of the car like a bronco out of a chute. We met at the end of the sidewalk and grabbed each other in a bear hug. Then we remembered how dumb we thought hugging was so we backed up and laughed.

Bobbi's Mom got out of the car then and walked up the walk to the house. My Mom met her halfway. I knew she didn't want her to come in because it was washday and she didn't like anyone to come in on washday. I was also aware that Mom had never, not once, invited Mrs. Keller into our house in the two years that they lived across the street. As far as I knew Mom had never been in the Keller's house, either.

Mrs. Keller stood there in front of my Mom, lighting up a cigarette and blowing smoke out the corner of her mouth. I knew Mom was not going to invite her in then. A smoking father was one thing, but a smoking mother? They stood together in that weird stiff way grown ups do when they don't like each other but don't want to admit it. Finally, Mrs. Keller said, "Well, I'll come back for Bobbi around 4:00."

She looked at us and said it again, as if we couldn't hear or understand the language she used when she talked to Mom. "I'll come back for you around 4:00, okay?"

"Okay!" Bobbi answered, and then she grabbed my hand

and started to run. We were off like startled colts and suddenly it was as if she had never left.

Our play that day was as much like it had been the day we met as any two days could be. We raced and jumped and raced some more. I thought I was in heaven. No one else knew quite how to do this with such abandon as Bobbi did. The fabric of our imagination wore thin only once when I asked if she had remembered to bring the picture of the two horses that lived across the street from her house. She said there were no horses across the street from her house.

"God," she said, "I live in a city. It's not like this at all." Then she shook her head like a horse shaking off a fly and took off running again.

There have been moments in my life where everything becomes suddenly clear to me. Where one piece of information settles into place and completes the whole picture. This was not one of those times. In fact, it made no sense to me at all, so I chose to ignore it. Even later, when I went back over everything Bobbi said to me, looking for clues of what eventually occurred, I still couldn't make sense of this. When she left me, she left me, and that may be all I'm ever going to know.

The world Bobbi left behind was no city. At night through our open windows we could hear crickets and frogs and freight trains that sounded their whistles but didn't slow down when they passed through on the south edge of town. Car traffic on main street, two blocks away, settled down to almost nothing by about 10:00 most evenings, though it picked up a little on Friday and Saturday nights when the bars closed. Trucks were the constant. Day or night you could always hear an eighteen-wheeler gearing up somewhere.

My Dad drove a truck and so did about half the fathers and older brothers of everybody I knew. The sound of that rising shifting whine can still get to me, especially at night. I hear it and think somebody's leaving home. Somewhere there's a little girl at a window, watching taillights.

Every time before my Dad left I would beg him to bring

home a horse for me. He hauled cattle so he had all the right equipment and went right up into the heart of cowboy country almost every week so how hard could it be to put just one horse in with the cows and bring it home? I explained how easy it would be for him to get the horse here and once it was here I could keep the horse in the playhouse out back. I would take care of it, I told him, honest I would.

This routine went on for years. Me begging, him ignoring. It got to be such a habit I forgot to stop when I realized I didn't really want a horse anymore. I came to that realization right before Christmas the year after Bobbi's first visit. I was writing a letter to her the moment it hit me. I remember writing, "Tonight, I'm going to tell my Dad he HAS to bring me a horse or I will die. I will. I know I'll die if I don't get a horse soon." As I re-read what I had written I realized it wasn't true. I wouldn't die if I didn't get a horse, I wouldn't even be all that upset.

Something about it scared me, I mean, who was I if I wasn't the lover of horses? I knew I was too tall to be racing around the yard kicking up my heels and pawing at the air with my fore hooves, but I still loved horses. Didn't I?

I was writing this letter to Bobbi when my Dad came home. As he sat at one end of the table pulling off his work boots I sat at the other writing my heart's desire as if by rote. I kept re-reading those words, "I'll die if I don't get a horse soon," and I couldn't even remember what it felt like to believe it. I felt older than I had ever felt before. My Dad sat across from me eating fried potatoes and chopped steak, oblivious to the change taking place across the table from him. The rest of the family had eaten hours ago, before Dad came home, so it was just he and I at the table. Mom was moving around the kitchen doing something that didn't interest me. Between bites he told her about his week. As was often the case, he would only be home long enough to eat, shower and refill his suitcase. This was the time I always made my plea. I let him leave the table and I put my letter in an envelope, licked it closed, and sat looking at it for a long time.

He was pulling on his coveralls before I said anything. He had the look of somebody already gone and I just wanted to say something to him to make this new feeling in me go away. I don't remember exactly what I said because it all came out in a rush, but my Mom heard the last part of it and the look on her face stopped me dead in my tracks.

"Don't ever say anything like that ever again!" she said. Dad didn't seem to hear either of us. He just kept leaving.

"I didn't mean I didn't want him to ever come home again," I whined. "I just want a horse really really bad."

"You! Go and think about what you just said." She turned her back on me and walked with Dad to the door. Good-byes were the only time I ever saw them kiss. This time she held on to his arm a little longer than usual, but other than that I figured it was just another night watching taillights.

When he didn't come home the night he was supposed to I knew it was my fault. I could hear my last words to him in my head, a refrain running over and under the memory of everything I had ever thought or done in my entire life.

"If you don't bring me a horse don't come home at all."

And he didn't come home. Mom was gone when I got up for school that day so I took care of myself. I poured a bowl of cereal, but I didn't eat it. My little sister and I walked to school together. She didn't know anything was wrong and I didn't know what was wrong so we walked in silence.

When you learn something like this from a stranger you remember odd things about the moment. Bob Thomsen wasn't really a stranger, but until that day he had never spoken to me or me to him. That morning I wasn't all the way in the classroom door before he was in front of me. He was wearing a green plaid button-down shirt and the top button was loose. Threads stuck out like little antennae.

"Hey," he said up close to my face. I could smell the peanut butter on his breath. "I hear your old man killed somebody."

"What?" I said.

"Yeah, it came over the police scanner this morning. My

Dad always turns it on first thing in the morning. Your Dad killed somebody with his truck." He looked almost puffed up with this information. "Deader'n a doornail."

Fear feels icy when it first comes but then it turns to fire and I could feel it creeping up my neck, onto my face. I can remember lifting up first one foot and then the other, as if walking was a newly learned skill. I walked to my desk and put my books down. A yellow No. 2 pencil with my teeth marks on it rolled out of the pencil slot and onto the floor. When I bent down to pick it up I felt my breath leave me and I couldn't remember how to get it back. I just kept going, slowly, until my whole body was on the floor beside the pencil. I didn't black out, I just forgot how to move.

They let me go home after that. They let me walk by myself the way they did in small towns in those days, and I found my way by staring straight ahead and letting my feet walk the familiar path. When I was about a block away from home I saw a glint of red in front of our house. I felt again the icy tingle up the back of my neck but this time it stayed icy until I got close enough to see my Dad's truck parked in front of the house. It looked naked somehow, without the trailer behind it, but it was there.

When I got home my Dad was sitting at the table, eating sausage and eggs and talking to my Mom. I could hear the low growl of his voice as I stepped onto the porch and somehow I knew when I stepped through the door his voice would stop. Like the war stories he never told, whatever had happened to him that night would join the silence of what looked like adulthood to me. I stood outside the kitchen door, my back pressed up against the cool stucco and listened to him tell my Mom what it felt like to be the instrument of what he called another man's suicide. "He came up behind me and drove under the trailer. I never even saw him." I heard him tell the whole story three times, each time he said, "I never even saw him," as if he couldn't quite believe his sense of sight had failed him so completely. When I opened the screen door and walked in they both looked at me with stricken faces. Where did I come from, they seemed to say, how did I get here? I didn't remember how to talk yet, and even if I did I wouldn't have known what to say. I felt closer to them than I ever had, but they didn't know that, so I just went into my bedroom and cried. For what, I didn't know.

The second time Bobbi came back for a visit I didn't need my Mom to warn me that Bobbi might be a little more mature than I was. Two years had passed since that first visit and I had changed some. I had started my period, had my first crush on a boy, and learned to live without horses. All that had happened to Bobbi too, but she was way beyond me.

Bobbi, who had written only about five letters in those two years, wasn't coming back alone. She was bringing a husband. I never did learn the whole story and trying to fit all the mismatched pieces of our letters and conversations didn't help. She didn't have to get married – I know because I had tactlessly blurted that question out when she called and arranged a time for a visit and gave me the big news.

Married? We were only fifteen. I hadn't even gone out on a date yet and she was married. What could I do with that kind of information? My mother wasn't much help. She remained as silent about this mystery as she did about her dislike for Bobbi's mother. She didn't seem all that surprised though. Her lips got tight when I told her and she didn't say anything at first, but when I kept talking about it, about how I just couldn't believe it, she said that the Keller family was "different." That's as far as she would go.

My new best friend, Janelle, was the one who first got me thinking about the possibility of this being a "Love Match."

"Maybe she just loves him so much that she can't live without him," she said when we were walking to school one morning. Janelle had never known Bobbi so her view of her could be anything she wanted it to be. I, on the other hand, had to work with my image of Bobbi as a wild horse in a young girl's body. Horses don't fall in love. They love their freedom, they love the wind, they love open spaces and green grass. But to fall in love, get married, be a wife. Who would have thought such a thing? Not me, I can assure you.

But I didn't have anything else to explain it, so along with Janelle I began to see Bobbi as some kind of romantic hero-ine. She was the first of my friends to fall under that deep mysterious spell of love and as such she became a romantic mystery herself. In the days before her visit I began to imag-ine her husband with the same kind of detailed, exacting day-dreams I had formerly limited to dreams of horses. Though any psychologist worth her salt would point out here that the leap from fantasizing about wild horses to imagining a friend's husband is a small and deeply related leap, I didn't see it that way. I didn't try to imagine their sexual life together. In fact, I spent most of the time thinking about them riding horses together, usually across some misty moor or along a deserted beach. That he would love horses was never in question for me. Of course he would. Bobbi hadn't changed that much I was sure.

The day she came was as cloudy and dreary as the first visit had been sunny and warm. This time Bobbi and her hus-band came for me. I wasn't waiting on the porch and when they pulled up Bobbi's husband honked the horn. They both stayed in the car and waited until I came out. I got in the back seat; Bobbi talked about almost everything under the sun from the minute I got in the car until the minute we got to the ranch where the Keller family was staying. I say she talked about almost everything: she didn't talk about her hus-band, she didn't talk to her husband, and she didn't tell me his name. When we got to the ranch she got out of the car and said to me, "Come on, I want you to see the horse we get to ride today." Her husband walked over to the fence, lit up a cigarette and watched us walk away.

It wasn't until we were on the horse, riding double, that I got up the courage to ask his name.

"Vincent," she said. "But I call him Vinnie." She touched her heels to the horse's flank and started off at a trot. "Man, this nag sure has a rough ride."

It was rough enough to keep me from asking any more questions, and, I guess that was the point.

When we got back to the corral Vinnie was still waiting by the fence.

"My turn," he said, and took the reins before we answered him. He jumped up onto the saddle without using the stirrup, sort of a Roy Rogers' move that would have been cool when we were twelve. I didn't look at Bobbi though so I don't know what she thought of it. I still thought he must be good with horses or Bobbi wouldn't have married him. I kept thinking that even when I saw him grab a switch from the willow tree at the edge of the corral. Surely he wouldn't use that on a horse, I thought. But he did. He started whipping the horse right in front of us and he was still whipping it when they disappeared from sight over the hill.

I looked at Bobbi, but she was studying something on her finger and didn't meet my eyes. Finally she said, "I'll show you where we're sleeping this week. It's kind of a cool little cabin."

We walked in silence toward a small building that must have at one time been a milk house. An old-fashioned separator still stood outside the door. Bobbi opened the door and pointed inside. I started to walk in but when I saw that all there was inside the building was a mattress on the floor covered with twisted up sheets and blankets I stopped in my tracks.

"Cool," I said, and backed away from the door. I don't know how many years it would take for me to figure out why that scene made me feel uncomfortable. I was, as my Mom recognized long ago, immature for my age. Truth be told, I think I still am. I seem to be walking through life one or two steps behind my peers. I have this feeling hanging over me that everyone else knows something I don't, has discovered the next stage before I'm completely finished with the one we're in. That's what it was about playing horses that I loved so much, that all my senses were so acute nothing got past me. I could see, hear, and smell the future and I knew what to do about it. When I raised my nose to the wind and whinnied the whole herd would follow me, and I always knew where to go. Oh, the thrill of knowing.

I honestly don't remember how long it was before Vinnie came back, and I don't remember what Bobbi and I did or what we talked about while we waited. All I really remember about the rest of the day was the sight of Vinnie racing toward us, still whipping that horse. He must have been only a few yards in front of us when he jerked up on the reins and stopped that poor horse. Mud shot up from its hooves and pink-tinged foam flew from its mouth. Vinnie leapt off the horse before it came to a complete stop. Bobbi and I just stood there; we didn't get out of the way or move to protect one another, our human senses so poor at preparing us for action. We weren't playing horses anymore.

I never saw Bobbi again after that day. The awkwardness in the car when they took me home hardened into a silence neither of us was able to break. Some how or another I learned that the Keller family had moved again, that Bobbi had moved with them, without Vinnie, but I never learned her new address.

The summer we turned eighteen, the summer before my last year of high school and the last year I lived in that little town, the Kellers came back for a visit. Bobbi didn't come that time. I learned of their visit when her mother came in to buy cigarettes in the store where I worked. I had already rung up her purchase and was handing back her change before we recognized each other.

"You're that girl who loved horses," she said.

I smiled my best customer service smile and asked her about Bobbi. She nodded and started walking away before she answered.

"Oh, Bobbi. She and her husband Dan moved up to Phoenix," she said over her shoulder. "They got jobs up there. I'll tell her I ran into you." The door swished shut behind her.

I watched her open a pack of cigarettes before getting into her car. The clear cellophane flittered across the parking lot, almost invisible. I pictured Vinnie, how he stopped that horse in front of us that day, the bit pulled tight against the softness of its mouth. When I played horses I knew how to take that bit in my teeth and though I had never seen a real horse do it I still believed it was possible. Bobbi's remarried, I thought. Man, I didn't see that coming, again.

It wasn't until Mrs. Keller's car pulled out of the parking lot that I remembered what she had said about me and horses. I watched her receding taillights until they were out of sight and thought about the time when that was true, when I was the girl who loved horses. "No," I finally said to myself. "I didn't just love horses." The slowness of my response bringing back the ache of something long since lost. "I didn't just love them."

DYANNA'S FACE
REFLECTED IN GLASS

I've been standing at this counter reading labels and studying packages for three, maybe four minutes. I'm trying to
decipher the marbleized pattern in each roast to identify
the "good" piece of meat my mother has sent me down here
to buy. I'm holding 4.39 pounds of meat. A Pike's Peak roast.
The name makes me laugh and I want to show it to Dyanna.

When I look up, I see her face reflected in glass at the
other end of the counter. Perhaps it's the distortion of the
glass that makes me suddenly feel as if I'm looking at her in
the future. We'll meet unexpectedly. She will have a daughter
who introduces herself to her mother's old friends. "I'm Julie.
Six years old," she will say, stating her age the way an older
version of herself would say a title or a degree. Dyanna will
introduce Julie's friend, a skinny, shy little girl who stands
behind Julie like a shadow. I will search Dyanna's face for
some sign she remembers we met in kindergarten, that we
once held hands like that.

Dyanna's face reflected in glass. Behind the image a white-
coated man deftly slices into a bloody mass of meat. A slab
peels away from the whole with each flash of steel. In front,
lines of neatly packaged, labeled cuts wait, ready to be picked

up and taken home by someone who wants them. Dyanna's face. Brown hair. Just brown. Not blonde or auburn or raven black. Brown, but thick. Thick, thick, thick. Masses of it around her face, over her shoulders, skimming her belt. With that hair I learned to braid. Dyanna between my knees, instructions ripped out of *Seventeen* propped between her back and my crotch. Ropes of hair as thick as my wrists twisted and contorted into shapes that looked only vaguely like what appeared on the page in front of me. She read aloud, "What Boys Look For," while I loved the feel of her hair in my hands.

I watch her now. She moves not quickly, but surely, along the cooler. What she picks up she puts into her cart, no reversal of decision once she touches a package or passes over another. She's been in charge of shopping for her family since she got her driver's license last year. It is one of the many jobs she shares with her sister. One of the jobs they had taken on in the way children do when the fabric of family disintegrates around them. "How do you know which one is good and which one isn't?" I ask.

"I just buy them." she answers with a shrug. "I don't care if anybody likes them when I put them on the table."

I decide on the roast in my hand, but don't show Dyanna the name on the label. With her in front of me it suddenly seems too childish.

"Mom wants me to get milk, bread, and a roast," I say as I tuck my selection into the corner of her cart.

"I'll meet you up front at the cash register, then. I need a few more things and we gotta hurry. If I don't get that car back before Dad gets home he'll kick my butt." She wheels the cart around and heads down an aisle away from me. I'm never sure if she's serious when she says things like this about her dad, she does not tell me the secrets of her family. But I have seen bruises and heard her silence. I hurry to get the milk and bread.

At her house we unload the groceries without talking. I set things out of the sacks and onto the counter for Dyanna to put away. It's not that I don't know where things belong. It's that I'm afraid someone will walk in while I am opening a cupboard. Her sister might ask me if I'm snooping. Her father might tell me to get the hell out of the cupboards. I don't know if they would do this, but the fear of it is enough to keep my hands away from the cupboard door knobs. I have been coming to this house once or twice a week for the past ten years and still it feels like a strange and alien country to me. Only in Dyanna's bedroom do I feel relaxed and welcome.

To get to that room we have to walk through the living room where venetian blinds and heavy drapes block out the late afternoon sun. Not until I am all the way into the room do I realize Dyanna's mother is sitting at the edge of the davenport, hunched over and, as always, smaller than I remember her.

"Are you doin' okay, Mom," Dyanna asks softly.

Mrs. Hunt looks up, startled by the sound.

"I didn't know you were home," she says in a voice deep and scratchy from years of cigarettes. She starts to cough and Dyanna stops beside her. I try to get out of the room before I hear the phlegmy rattle in her chest.

I shut the door to Dyanna's room quickly to block out the sound, and Dyanna's wedding gown, hanging on a hook on the back of the door, swings out and brushes against me. It is ivory linen, tea length, and simply styled, because Dyanna hopes to wear it again after her wedding for formal occasions on the army base in Germany.

I've known for four months Dyanna is getting married and leaving, yet the fact continues to surprise me whenever I see signs of her preparations. The boy she is marrying is tall and handsome and not afraid to kiss her in public. He calls her his "old lady" and Dyanna tells me he can't get enough of her. I cannot bring myself to like him, really like him. But I keep this feeling to myself. Dyanna, I think, believes I secretly envy her. Because I love her and this belief makes her happy I never let on that I don't.

I stand before the dress, a lump forms in my throat and suddenly I remember I have to get the groceries home. My hand reaches up to the lace inset at the neckline. The lace is beautiful and fragile-looking but rough to the touch. I trace the outline of the inset and a hidden stick pin pricks my finger. Horrified that I may have bled on Dyanna's dress, I stand on tiptoes, sucking my wounded finger, studying the dress for any sign of red. The door opens suddenly, hits me in the face, and the dress falls onto my head. I stumble backward, trying to get out of the way of the door and get the dress off my head. I hear Dyanna laughing but before I see how funny this all is another stick pin rakes the side of my face and this time I am sure I will stain her dress. I shriek and throw the dress away from me. Dyanna falls onto the bed laughing.

"You look so funny!" she screams.

"I ruined your dress!" I scream back, holding my right hand over my stinging cheek and trying to pick the dress up off the floor.

"No you didn't. It just fe . . . Oh my god your cheek! What happened?" She leans close to my face while I search the dress again for some sign that I have ruined her wedding.

"One of the stick pins got me," I say and hold the dress up to the light. "I don't see anything on it, do you?"

"Don't worry about it. I'm going to have it dry cleaned after it's finished."

"God, Dyanna, I'm sorry."

"What are you sorry about? Look at your face!"

I turn to the mirror above the dresser. The reflection of my face hovers over a ballerina balancing on a jewelry box. I see a red curve from my jaw to the corner of my eye. The pin had slid under the skin, creating a swath effect across my face but opening only a small line where tiny drops of blood have formed.

"Oh shit. I look like an idiot."

"Jesus, doesn't that hurt?

"No. Yeah. Not really," I say as I lean close to the mirror.

"It looks like it hurts," Dyanna says as she turns away to hang the dress back on the door. "Do you want a wash cloth or anything?"

"No." I turn from the mirror and watch her smooth the folds of the dress carefully. The way she caresses it I imagine she is seeing herself in it, seeing herself beside Boyd right now. I'm surprised by a sudden stinging of tears in my eyes and I know I have to get out the door before Dyanna sees. "I gotta get home," I say.

As always she walks me to the corner between our two houses. She talks from the moment the back door slams behind us until we reach the corner, giving me time to hide from my thoughts.

"I have to fix supper tonight and I know that witch sister of mine won't be around to clean up the dishes so I can't be ready till at least 7:30. I'll call you right before I leave. Meet me and I'll bring my stuff over to your house."

I nod while she tells me our plan. It will not matter what is going on at home, what my mother says, or who else needs me. I will be ready when Dyanna calls.

"We can walk out to the Texaco from your house. I told Boyd to meet us there cause if my old man sees Boyd's car anywhere near your house when I'm spending the night there I'm dead." She fishes a cigarette from her purse as she talks and looks up and down the street before she lights it. "He's just frantic his little girl is going to get laid before her wedding. Shit." She exhales sharply through her nose. "Boyd said he would bring Robert along if you wanted him to."

"Oh sure," I say, rolling my eyes. "I'll pass." Boyd's supply of friends available for doubling is dwindling and though Dyanna would never admit this about any of Boyd's friends, we both know that Robert, of the prematurely receding hair line and bad breath, would be scrapping the bottom of the barrel. "Mom is only letting me go to this party 'cause she thinks since its a wedding dance there'll be enough adults around to keep me 'safe'. Besides, I promised if she let me go I would quit bugging her about letting me date until after my birth-

day. Only one month to go." It is a source of major embarrassment to me that my mother will not allow me to date until I
am sixteen while my best friend, who is only ten months older
than I am, is making wedding plans. Even more painful to me
than my mother's rules is the fact that I have not yet had to
turn down a date that was not set up by Dyanna.

"If Mom finds out I snuck out on another date she won't
even let me come to your wedding." We are parting, walking
backwards in opposite directions when I say this. As soon as
the words are out of my mouth my eyes start stinging again.

"See ya after supper," I say and turn my back to her.

I tell myself it's okay that I'm not going to be Dyanna's
maid of honor. I know why she asked her sister instead of me.
I know her mother cried and told her it would make her so
happy to see her two little girls standing on the altar together.
I understand about family. But Dyanna is my Best Friend. I
have loved her best almost all of my life. The day she told me
I would have to sit with the rest of the congregation and
watch her get married I felt as if I had loved alone all these
years.

She asked me to be her maid of honor the very day Boyd
asked her to marry him. Before she told anyone else. I
helped her choose the pattern for her dress. I helped her
choose her colors. But then something happened at home.
She wouldn't tell me when I was supposed to go in to be
measured for my dress. One day in my room I asked her
about the wedding. I didn't ask her about what I would be
doing, I just asked about the food and Dyanna started crying.
Sitting on my bed she started crying. I knelt down in front of
her and she told me.

"It's not just my Mom," she said. "It's my Dad, too. He
said if I didn't want to listen to my Mom I could get my ass
out of his house right now." She kept wiping tears away, but
her voice never broke. "Don't you see, Jenny? I just gotta finish high school and if Dad kicks me out I can't. Boyd's folks
won't let him marry me if I don't finish high school. Don't
you see, Jenny? I just gotta stay. Just a few more months." It

wasn't until that moment that I knew how badly she wanted to get away and I knew I would do anything to help her.

I put my arms around her waist and just held on to her. I felt her sobbing and I felt so small. I wanted so badly to help her, but I knew of nothing I could do. I hated to think it was anything but love that made her want to go to a country that was farther away than either of us had ever dreamed of going.

One month from tomorrow, the day after her wedding, Dyanna will get on a plane and fly away. Soon I will be seeing Dyanna's handwriting on an airmail envelope with a foreign postmark. Nothing I have ever read or heard or thought can help me picture Dyanna there. I can't see the countryside, the buildings, the people. I can only imagine signs of Dyanna coming back to me across the miles. I do not want to think about it. Tonight she is staying with me.

The wedding dance is in a barn on a farm fifteen miles north of town. I will be much older and living in a city on the east coast before I realize that wedding dances held in cleaned out barns or Quonset huts are not the norm. But for now it does not occur to me that dancing the Cotton-Eyed Joe in the milk cow holding pen is an odd way to celebrate a new marriage.

When we first got here Boyd took off with a group of the groom's friends and left Dyanna and me on our own. I was happy to see him go. I was afraid they would dance every dance while I stood outside the halo of light and watched.

But now it is just Dyanna and me, listening to the people and watching everything. The night's warm air blesses everything around us. I feel the music like a prayer. Inside the barn, bright lights strung along the rafters cast an unreal glow on the dancers. Shadows flickering in time to the music reach up to the ceiling along the walls and back into the darker recesses of the barn. Outside the double barn doors, at the edge of the circle of lights, folding chairs hold blue-haired women and overweight men. A group of mostly young men hover around the keg set up in the back of a pick-up.

Because I'm looking for someone in white it is a while

before I recognize the bride. She is wearing blue jeans, a red tank top and a massive wrist corsage composed of red roses and white daisies. It is the corsage that sets her apart from the other young women her age. She dances almost every dance, first with men who could be her father and then with boys who could be her son. No matter how awkward her dance partner, she keeps smiling and I wonder what she is thinking. When the groom claims a dance with her she keeps smiling.

Maybe it is something about the light, or the moon, or the music. But tonight something is different. I can feel it. I am standing by the car with Dyanna and a tall blonde man walks over to me. He asks me my name. He smiles at me and talks to me. To me. Not Dyanna. I am tongue-tied with surprise, but I smile back at him. I laugh when he does. When he asks me to dance with him I look at Dyanna to see if I heard him right. He puts his hand on my elbow and guides me to the dance area. The band is playing a slow dance and before I can tell him I don't know how to dance he takes me into his arms and we move slowly around in a circle. For the first time in my life I feel the way I imagine a beautiful girl feels.

When the dance is over I go back to stand beside Dyanna, but before the music starts another boy I don't know asks me to dance. I catch Dyanna's eye and we both laugh. We don't have to talk to know what we would say to one another.

It is some time before I see her again. When I do Boyd is back and he is holding her close. The way he touches her in front of all these people makes my face warm so I don't approach them until I know it is time to go home. I can see on her face that she has something to tell me. Something she knows I won't want to hear and I feel the night slipping away.

"Jean's mom asked me if I could hang around and help put away food," she says.

"We have to be home by midnight," I answer. I know she knows this.

"Yeah, well, um, Boyd's mom and dad are out of town tonight and I kinda thought I would stay with him."

I feel myself crumbling. I have so much I want to tell her

about tonight. She has a lifetime with Boyd ahead of her. We have so little time left. "When did you find out about Boyd's folks?"

She looks out into the darkness away from me.

"Thursday."

I feel my stomach tighten. "Oh."

I turn away from her and watch the people mill around.

"How am I supposed to get home if you're staying here?"

"Boyd said he would give you a ride and then come back to get me. Will that be all right?"

I know she has already made up her mind, so I shrug my shoulders in a way that might mean yes.

When I get into the car with Boyd I bump my head on the door frame. Before I realize how stupid it sounds I mumble, "Sorry." Then I laugh and try to pretend it didn't happen. God, I can't believe I thought I was graceful when I was dancing. Boyd doesn't appear to notice my awkwardness.

"Nice night," he says.

I nod.

"Isn't it?"

"Oh. Yeah." I squeak. I didn't know he wanted me to answer. When he pulls away from the other parked cars he guns the engine and the back end of the car fish tails as we head down the gravel drive. When we get to the end of the drive he takes the corner too short and both wheels on the passenger side sink into the soft gravel stockpiled at the edge of the road. The car bogs down for a moment and Boyd puts the gas pedal down to the floor. We shoot across the road and for a second I think we're going to end up in the opposite ditch, but he swings the car around just in time and brings us back to the center of the road.

"Whoa. I think I went overboard on the schnapps sipping tonight. I'm going to skip taking the highway home, just in case John Law is out. Side roads okay with you?"

I nod.

"Are they okay?" he asks.

"Oh. Yeah." I squeak again. I hate it when I squeak and I

feel like an idiot. I tell myself to just relax. It's just Boyd. As he drives he keeps looking over at me. I try to think of something to say to him but my mind is a complete blank.

He puts his arm on the back of the seat and I don't really think about it being nearer to me. My dad drives like that. Men drive like that. They spread out and take room when they drive. When he asks if it is okay for him to have his arm there I say it is.

"I can't hear you way over there. Move over a little bit so we don't have to shout at each other," he says.

"I'm not shouting," I answer.

"What?"

"I'm not shouting," I say again only louder. He laughs at me. Maybe I am being stupid. I wish Dyanna were here because she knows what to do and I could just do what she does. But she isn't here and Boyd is laughing at me. "I'm not going to bite you," he says. "I just can't hear you way over there." So I slide over a little bit. It is okay. He just keeps driving and talking about going into the army.

When he stops talking the car is so quiet I can hear my stomach growl. I have to say something.

"That's Orion's Belt up there," I blurt, pointing at the sky.

"Where?" He stops the car. I start to slide back across the seat, but his right arm tightens around my shoulders. "Don't run away. We're just looking at stars. You sure spook easy."

So I stay where I am. He stops looking at the stars and starts looking at me. My heart starts to beat faster.

"You look really nice tonight. I saw you out there dancing. I never noticed how pretty you're getting to be. " His finger lightly traces the scratch down the side of my face. "Even all scarred up." He puts his finger under my chin and tilts my face upward. His face is so close to mine I can't breathe. He lightly kisses my nose. Then, slowly, he kisses my lips. I am too surprised to turn away until he pushes his tongue inside my mouth. I pull my head back and then his hand touches my stomach, under my shirt. I try to push it away but it slides up and cups my breast. I push his hand harder away from me and he lets me, but when I try to slide away from him his right arm tightens around my shoulders and his left hand slides up, under my skirt. He presses his finger against the fabric of my underwear then slides under and touches me down there. I want to deny this. I want to say I screamed and struggled all the time, but for just that second, I let him touch me. I never had a man touch me there and for just that moment I let it happen. But then I know this is wrong. I tell him no. No. I push him away but his arms tighten around me. For the first time I realize the smell in the car is the smell of alcohol on his breath. For the first time I realize the danger. I pull away and try to pull my skirt down. He watches me with narrowed eyes, his breath rapid and uneven.

"You don't have a bra on," he says. He reaches over so fast I think he is going to strike me. My hand shoots up to protect my face and he grabs my shirt and pulls it open.

"Don't!" I try to pull my shirt around me. He grabs my leg, pulls me toward him and pushes me down onto the seat. Then his knee is between my legs, he pushes me across the seat. I try to stop him. I tell him no. No. But he doesn't hear me. He holds my hands back and pulls hard at my underwear, so hard the seam on the side rips. Then he is on top of me, pushing into me. He feels like a knife between my legs and I scream and scream. I try to get away but he just keeps thrusting into me. My head is twisted against the door handle and he holds my wrists together across my neck. I cry and beg him to stop but he just keeps hurting me. I close my eyes as tight as I can and try to twist my hips away from the pain but he shoves his weight into me and I can't get away.

And then he is finished. The weight of him crushes me and I cannot move. Finally he pulls away from me and turns on the dome light. I try to cover myself, but my leg is pinned behind him against the seat.

"Christ, you're a virgin," he says. "What a fuckin' mess."

I pull away into a curl on the floor and fumble until I find the door latch. I crawl out of the car and close the door against the harsh circle of light. I squat, leaning against the car. I feel my blood and his semen running out of me. I feel the cold steel of the car against my forehead and I squat there. I want to cry, but no tears will come to my eyes.

I hear him roll down the car window.

"Do you want a Kleenex?" he says. I hear myself say yes, but I don't know how I make the words come out. My hand reaches up and touches the white mass he hands me. I try to wipe myself but it hurts so badly I can only touch myself lightly. I creep around to the back of the car. I'm so afraid he will see me. I can't get my panties untangled and try and try and try.

Inside the car he is quiet for so long I think maybe he has passed out. I think maybe I can run away from the car and get home. I start to look around, to see where I can hide, but before I can run he gets out of the car and comes to where I am. I crouch down and try to hide myself from him. He has a cigarette in his hand and he sits down beside me. I start to move away from him, but he reaches out and grasps the back of my neck. I can't move.

"Are you crying?" he says. "Christ. I didn't know you were a virgin." He takes a drag of his cigarette. "I never had a virgin before." He takes another long drag of his cigarette then flicks it toward the middle of the road. "You should've told me." He stands up. "You just should've told me."

"If you want a ride, let's go."

I stay there on the ground, crouched, trying to hide myself. He starts the car and I hear him yell something. Then he comes around to the back of the car.

"Do you want me to put you in the car myself."

I get into the car. I get into the car with him. I lean against the door, riding in the car with him. I am so afraid he will stop again, that he will touch me if I make a sound, I hold onto the door handle and press myself against the door as far away from him as I can.

When we get to my house I open the door before he stops the car. I run up onto my lawn and he drives away. I lean against the rough gray bark of the cottonwood in my front yard. I slide down, crouching and crying against the tree. I can't go inside. But someone will see me here. They will find me here and they will know.

I have to go inside. I have to hide. In the bathroom I lock the door behind me and I don't turn on the light. I feel along the tub and find the plug and push it into the drain. I turn on the water, hot. I hear it rushing out of the faucet and I feel the steam rising. In the cupboard I push aside towels until I find the Kotex. I empty them out into the cupboard and pull out the sack. I take off my clothes, roll them up and put them in the sack. Then I push it to the bottom of the trash can.

I step into the tub. The water burns my skin. I sink down into the water and let myself burn.

In the dim light from the window I see the water rippling. It is then that I think of her. I imagine Dyanna's face reflected in the water. I can't bear to look at it and I sink down into the water, willing it to cleanse me. I can't tell her he did this to me. She will hate me. She will never forgive me. I can't let her go away with him. She will go to a country where no one knows her. Where no one loves her. He will hurt her. I know this. She will go away and I will never see her again. If she stays, it will be in her father's house. She will hate me she will never forgive me. I sink down into the water and I wish for this life to stop. Just stop.

THE THING ABOUT FLYING

See, the trick is you have to hold your leg out in front of you as straight as you can and keep your arms outstretched, you know, kind of like rotors. Then you spin in circles. It sounds hard, I know, because you're only on that one leg and all, but it is that other leg stretched out in front of you that is the ticket, the key, the very secret of it all. If all it took were sticking your arms out and spinning kids would be clogging the skies because kids are always sticking out their arms and spinning. It's what kids do in backyards and on street corners all over the world. But what they don't know is that you have to hold one leg out in front of you, straight as you can, and then stick out your arms and spin in circles.

At first all you can do is kind of hop in a circle. You'll feel stupid and you'll look stupid, but don't let that stop you. It's worth it to keep trying. Just keep hopping. If you keep at it you'll pick up some speed and pretty soon your hop will be more of a pirouette and then all of a sudden you're off. The first couple of times when you first lift off you'll feel like you're falling over and you'll probably put your foot down too soon and you'll have to start over, but just trust yourself that you won't fall over. People who don't learn to trust themselves don't learn to fly, so keep that foot out there even when you think you're going to hit the ground. So what if you hit the ground? You've hit it before and you'll hit it again so don't waste any time worrying about that. Worry about things that matter, like the bully on the bus who keeps picking on your son or about your nephew on a peacekeeping mission in Kosovo or the overcrowded under-funded school you send your daughter off to every morning, but don't worry about hitting the ground. Sometimes you will and sometimes you won't and worrying about it only makes this harder.

Now once you're up a few feet in the air you can relax that leg and let it down slowly, but keep your arms out until you're really up there. They'll be what guide you and you don't want them pointing down. Trust me on that one. Once you're up there you'll feel you've been flying your whole life and you'll wonder why you haven't been. The expanse of sky is so blue it's like swimming in the eye of God. The air up there is so fine and warmer than you'd expect. It might even remind you of the womb.

When you look back at your house and yard—and you will...—because everybody does, you'll see your kids, your friends, and everybody you've ever loved or known. Now here's something you need to know: for one scary minute you won't remember a single thing about them. This is where a lot of people fail. They think it's forever. They think they're alone. They drop their hands and fall right out of the sky. Don't let this happen to you. You're terrestrial. Learning to fly won't change that so just enjoy yourself. When you get back down you'll still be you, just a you that knows how to fly.

Eventually everybody comes back down. That's a given. The hard part is holding on to the feeling of flying even when both your feet are back on the ground. This is the part I didn't tell you before: once you've been up there you have to want to go back, really want to go back. Wishful thinking or half-hearted dreaming won't get you there. You have to want it in your heart and your head and to the very tip of every one of your fingers and toes or else all the trick spinning in the world won't get your heavy old self off the ground again. This part sounds easy, but it's not, and that's the thing about flying that most people never get. That's why there are so few people up there. It's like any kind of success. It looks easy, but it's not.

NIGHT SOUNDS

She watched her father's hands as he stabbed his fork into a piece of bread and spread it thickly with margarine and jelly. Like his arms and the V-patch on his neck, his hands were deep red, permanently burned by too many hours in the sun. The tips of his fingernails were grease-stained black crescent moons. Scars and abrasions marked his knuckles and fingers. If asked, he would not be able to say how the injuries got there. He had no time for minor things.

She remembered once when he had fallen while working in the field and broken a bone in his left foot. He had fastened two large pipe-wrenches together so that he could work the clutch by hand and keep going until nightfall. By the time he got back to the house his foot was so swollen her mother had to slit his boot down the sides and peel it off. The doctor said later the flow of blood had been cut off so long that he was lucky he didn't lose his foot.

"Had to get the corn in," he had replied.

Katie remembers standing in the corner of the kitchen watching his face as her mother worked, bent over his foot. Her face had grown hot when she realized she was waiting, wanting, to see him wince, just once.

Tonight what she wanted was to see him smile. She wanted to see the wrinkles at the corners of his eyes deepen and his gray eyes soften. It was a look she had seen on his face many times but she seldom saw him turn it on her. Sometimes she would feel his eyes on her and she would feel trapped, exposed in his gaze. When she would look up his eyes would move on, as if he hadn't found what he was looking for. She never knew what it was that he wanted and he never said. She had learned to expect his distance, but tonight she wanted it to be different.

"Tomorrow we'll go fishing," he had said that morning. Her brothers had whooped in excitement and began to make plans. Nothing needed to be said for her to know that she was not included. The lines were clear in her family, and in the world, at that time. Each member had his or her place and Katie was seldom included with her brothers.

After breakfast, the boys rattled down the driveway chattering about the plans for the day and Katie helped her mother with dishes. As soon as the last dish was in the cupboard, Katie rushed out the back door. She longed for open spaces so she headed for the pastures, away from the house and the roads. She kept her eyes downcast and her feet automatically followed the trails the cattle had made over the years. The land looked flat from a distance but the trail she walked moved up and down small rolling hills. It dipped into deep hollows that hid everything but the blue cloudless sky overhead and then rose again so quickly that she would sometimes feel as if she were standing on top of the world. Everything seemed just beyond the horizon that lie miles and miles away from her, from that moment.

Tomorrow her dad and brothers were going up north to the river. They were going some place and doing something and Katie was to stay home. Suddenly a feeling of energy, of desire, welled up inside her and she began to run. Her feet left the trail and headed out across the grassland. She ran and ran until her lungs felt as if they would burst. She stumbled and fell to her knees, but the feeling was so strong it made her feel as if she were racing even as she crouched there on the ground. She pulled herself up and kept moving forward. Her steps were heavy and she gasped for air. Finally her heart stopped pounding against her rib cage and her breathing returned to normal. She stopped walking and looked around her. She was still there in the pasture owned by her father and her grandfather and she was no closer to the horizon. Everything was the same. Her feet could fly over this ground but she was still a bird without wings.

She helped her brothers dig worms at the edge of the garden before she went in to help with supper. They laughed when she said she wanted to go along with them in the morning.

"You don't even know how to bait a hook," James said.

"I do too," she replied. "I've watched you do it." How could he know what she knew, she thought. He simply shrugged and told her to bring the pail closer. Her brothers would not be her allies.

Her mother didn't laugh when she told her. At first she didn't say anything at all. She stopped slicing bread for a moment and gazed out the window. Katie knew she understood how important this could be, but she also knew that didn't mean she would help. "Do you think he'll let me go?" she asked quietly.

"I don't know, Katie," she said. "Men need time with their sons." She stepped into the pantry quickly, almost as if fleeing from her daughter's questions.

"But what about his daughter?" Katie whispered to the stack of plates in her hands.

During supper she struggled to find the words to move her father. The weight of his expected answer seemed to push her down in her chair, but he hated it when she slumped so she tried to hold her head up and sit with her back straight. Her head felt so heavy whenever she looked up and saw his face. His eyebrows were dark and thick and his jaw too strong. She knew how quickly his face could change to anger.

It made her afraid when she tried to look at him. Finally she inhaled deeply, breathing in courage.

"Dad, can I go along tomorrow?" There. She said it. She tried to bring her eyes up to look at his face, but could only get as far as the package of Camels in his right front pocket.

"Go fishing?" he said between bites. "Kind of a funny thing for you to want to do."

Her brothers paid no attention to her question and went on with their stories. They had been to the neighbor's ranch that morning to help with the branding. Their eyes still held the glow of the branding iron as they competed with each other to tell the best part of the day.

He listened to them. He asked them questions. He laughed with them.

He hadn't said no, she thought. She stirred her mashed potatoes and flattened them smooth with her spoon. With the tine of her fork she wrote, "Please," faintly, before taking a bite.

"Did you finish your book today, Katie?" She heard her mother's words as if they were a rope thrown out to someone struggling against a current. Katie looked into her mother's face as into a refuge.

"Yes," she said. "It was so cool. It was about this beautiful horse that could jump the highest fences."

"What's its name? Frog?" her brother's voice cut in.

"Yeah, and in the end, it croaks," the other said. They laughed at their own cleverness. Katie stopped. Her story could wait.

Her father was finished eating and had taken a toothpick from the jar. Before he could push away from the table Katie again breathed in her courage.

"Can I, Dad? Can I go along with you tomorrow?"

"I think your mother probably needs help around here," he said. Katie turned to her mother and waited. Would she help her?

"I'm not doing anything I can't handle alone," her mother said casually as she started stacking plates. Katie wanted to kiss her right then and there but instead she turned back to her father. She had never gone fishing before and she didn't know if she would like it, but her brothers liked it and that was enough to make her want to try. She didn't understand the rules that kept her from joining her brothers. She didn't believe it was a difference in age. She was less than two years younger than Mark and sometimes she felt that she was the oldest.

She thought about the day Mark had found a snake in the basement. He had raced up the stairs two at a time screaming as if he had seen a demon. He and Katie were the only ones home so there was no need to hide his fear. Katie went out to the shed and got a hoe and went down the steps with it held tightly in her hands. She felt as cold-blooded as the enemy she faced as she walked from room to room. Suddenly she heard, or felt, a movement in the back of the storage room. She pulled the door shut behind her and moved toward the sound. With the hoe still raised in her right hand she pulled a box full of old clothes out away from the wall and with her foot pushed another box closer to the brick foundation. There, curled up in the corner, was the snake, a bull snake, not a rattler as her brother had claimed. For a moment she watched it, its head darting back and forth searching for an escape, its body sliding gracefully over and under itself. She could almost feel its fear and she felt her resolve weaken. But then the snake dropped its head and moved straight toward her. She raised the hoe high and brought it down on the snake, almost severing its head.

She had never killed anything before and she felt excited and frightened when she saw how easy it was. When the snake's body stopped moving, she carried it up the steps draped over the end of the hoe. She loved the admiration in her brother's eyes almost as much as she loved the sense of power she felt.

When her father came home that night Mark rushed out to tell him about the snake he had found in the basement. But engine trouble on the tractor that day had put her father behind on his harvest and his temper was short. Katie stepped out of the back door just as her father's eyes came to rest on the hoe leaning against the stoop.

"Who left that damn hoe out again?" he asked angrily. She stood there guiltily, unable to answer him.

"What's wrong with you, girl?" he shouted at her. "Do you think things will just take care of themselves? Can't you take a little responsibility around here?"

She shrank before her father's anger. No one told him about the snake, or what she had done. Even she began to believe there was nothing special about the story.

When her brothers jumped up from the supper table and headed upstairs and her father reached for the paper Katie could feel her chance slipping away.

"I really want to go along, Dad."

"What?" he said, as if he had already forgotten what she was asking for. He usually read the paper quickly and efficiently after supper and he didn't like to be slowed down by interruptions. "Go along?" He turned to page two and scanned the headlines. "We're leaving awfully early. You'll never get up in time." He didn't look up from the paper so, to his credit, he never saw how important his answer was to her. "If you get up by yourself, I don't care."

Katie rushed into the kitchen and threw her arms around her mother.

"Don't get so excited," her mother said. "You've never gotten up that early. You may not wake up in time." She stroked Katie's hair and then pushed her away.

But Katie knew she could. She could already see herself sitting beside her father on the dock – would there be a dock? They would cast out their lines and then her father would lazily light a cigarette and squint up at the few clouds in the sky. He would ask her if she thought thy would get any rain tonight. She would look seriously up at the sky and say, "Maybe, maybe not." And her father would laugh because that's just what he would say. He would suddenly realize they were so very much alike. Then the bobber on Kate's line would go under once, twice, and then stay under and with a jerk Katie would reel it in. Maybe it wouldn't be the biggest fish, but it would be big enough to keep and her father would say, "Good job, Katie," or "Looks like fried fish for supper tonight," or maybe he wouldn't say anything at all. Maybe he would just put his hand on her shoulder and smile at her.

So many images of how right tomorrow would go kept flickering through her mind. A little girl's dreams can be so simple, so complex. She wrapped herself in her thoughts and avoided her father for the rest of the evening, afraid that if he saw her he would change his mind.

In the dark of the next morning she heard her father's steps as he moved softly around his bedroom and then across the hall to where her brothers lay sleeping. Katie sat up on the edge of the bed and her excitement made her heart race as she fumbled to pull off her pajamas.

She had done it. She was awake in time to go along. She had stayed awake and listened to the house go to sleep around her. She had seen the moon sink behind the trees and she had watched a star fall out of the patch of sky outside her window. Again and again the night sounds of crickets and clocks had lulled her to sleep, but each time she had jerked herself awake. Now she could feel the coolness of the pre-dawn air on her skin and she shivered. She was awake, she could go along. She yawned and wanted to laugh out loud, but just as her hand touched the doorknob, she heard her father's voice say quietly, "Hold it down, boys. You'll wake your mother and sister."

She felt time stop and her excitement drain from her. She sat back down on the edge of her bed and looked down at the dirty white tennis shoe she held in her right hand. She touched the hole her toe had made in the flimsy canvas. Then she set it down neatly beside its mate. Slowly she lay back down. She felt the pills on the sheet rub against her leg as she pulled her knees up to her chest. She closed her eyes tight and tried to swallow.

In the kitchen her brothers whispered excitedly and then the back door slammed. It seemed to Katie that it was she who was drifting away from their sounds, the way a leaf on the water drifts away from a boat. When the pickup crunched down the gravel drive passed her window, Katie rolled onto her back and watched as the morning light filled her room.

DIAMOND

Before Ramsay stepped off the curb at the corner near her childhood home, the March wind lifting a wisp of her brown hair, wrapping it across the bridge of her nose and covering her hazel eyes, before she looked down at a stubborn patch of ice hidden in the shadow of the curb, her brown leather hiking boots negotiating its slippery surface, and before, of course, Michael White, age sixteen, threw back the last of the bottle of Jack Daniels he had stolen from the cupboard above his father's refrigerator, its amber warmth burning his eyes, his throat, his stomach, and slid behind the wheel of his mother's '85 red Taurus, gunned the engine, shoved in a cassette of White Snake's latest release, before he turned the corner onto the street of Ramsay's childhood home, suddenly feeling the rush of music and liquor and youth, and anger, too, at the slowness of life, finally letting it all come together in the swift pressure of his right foot causing his car to leap forward catching Ramsay's left hip with the right front corner of that car, before she sailed across the windshield, Michael's face through the glass not yet registering shock, before her body continued its graceful arc across the roof of his car, landing $35^1/_2$ feet away from that stubborn patch of ice, her head the first part of her twenty-nine year-old body to return to the ground, striking first the curb then the still-brown grass, the rest of her twisting and turning and coming to rest in a strangely natural-looking position on that grass not yet green, as if she had chosen to take a nap just there, just then, before the blood began to seep from the nose her friend Emily had said made her look more patrician than any young woman from a small town in North Dakota had the right to look, yes, before the choreography of that, Ramsay's last moments, was set into motion, she and Emily had been friends.

To mention Emily now, in the hour, in the very minute of Ramsay's death, you will think that Ramsay and Emily were more than friends, that barring some blood relationship they were lovers, openly or secretly, that they had exchanged some bodily fluid and thus sealed some pact, moving them up the hierarchy of relationships, but no, they were just friends. Best friends. Bosom buddies. Soul mates. Two peas in a pod. Two of a kind. Birds of a feather. Two lonely people too much in love to say good night. No, not in love, see how easy it is to make that mistake? Loving, caring, needing even, but not "in love." Just friends. That we must know, must accept, before we move on into the story of a friendship that ended – did not end – early one spring in Ramsay's hometown, 759 miles away from the city where she had lived since starting college some ten years before.

The week before she left that city for the last time was a week not unlike most weeks, or so it seemed at the time. Days trudge on, one after another, looking so much the same you think life, like friendship, doesn't change until you look back and realize it is not, cannot be, the same at the beginning as it is at the end. We come into any relationship not so much pure as the result, the accumulation, of all our previous relationships – from gene pool to lovers. Still we come ready, whether we know it or not, to be touched, changed.

And on what are these relationships, these friendships based? Love? Respect? Proximity? Tell me. I want to know.

This friendship is so common, so familiar, so filled with un-events. It's as if you can look at these two and know why recorded history has left out the lives of women. Nothing happens that you can see. These are not war stories; there is no bonding in fire. Knowing that, I keep looking at them, wanting to make sense of this connection that runs so deep.

See these two early in their friendship, on their thirty-fifth night sharing a 15' x 20' dorm room. Emily sits with her right foot propped up on the desk, her left leg scrunched before her on the chair. Her cropped blonde hair swings forward as she dips the brush into the bottle of Crazy Cranberry nail polish and leans toward her foot. Precise as a surgeon she applies the bright polish to her little toe, pauses to adjust the cotton between her long, slender toes, then dips the brush again.

Ramsay lies propped against all the pillows on her bed, a textbook open on chest. She watches Emily's movements.

"You look like a guy having sex," Ramsay says.

"What?!" Emily replies. Her brush stops in mid air.

"Oh, you know," Ramsay says. "You're concentrating so hard. Your tongue's practically sticking out of the corner of your mouth and your brow's all furrowed. You just look like a guy who's trying to cum."

"Gawd. What a weird thing to say." Emily puts the brush back into the bottle and wipes her hand across her brow as if to smooth it. Saying "gawd" is the closest Emily comes to cursing, so you know Ramsay's comment has touched her somewhere deep.

"Oh come on now," Ramsay says. "Don't go all Catholic girl on me. I've got your number."

"Well," Emily replies. "You don't have everything." She reaches down to adjust the cotton between her toes and tucks her chin so Ramsay can no longer see her face.

Ramsay sits up, pulls a pillow around to her chest and hugs it. "Oh come on now," she says again. "What are you holding back? Give me the dirt, the real dirt and nothing but the dirt." It's not that she doesn't honor Emily's way, it's just that she has set out to be someone new here in this new town, this new stage of her life, and this newness includes her own improvised view of confidence. She will never again be the hesitant child, the quiet adolescent. In her own quest for the new self she doesn't yet recognize the thin ice signs of someone who feels everything beneath the surface. Someone like Emily.

Emily paints her third and fourth toes in silence. Ramsay perches at the edge of the bed, waiting. If the phone hadn't rung right then Emily might not have told her any more. She might have said no, that door's closed to you, and by saying it making it so, but the phone rings, the conversation is interrupted, the danger passes.

As it is, the door is left open, and when they come to it again, they walk through it. Later that night – or was it the next night? – when they come home from separate dates, both feeling the effects of alcohol, Ramsay comes back to it again.

"So did you get laid?"

"Gawd Ramsay, do you have to be so crude?" A slight flush creeps up Emily's neck, though she's not as put off by Ramsay's question as you might suspect. In fact, she's beginning to like the freedom, the no-holds-barred attitude she sees in Ramsay's conversation.

"Oh, sorry," Ramsay says, obviously not sorry at all. "I just wanted to know if you watched his face. You know how I said they get this look of concentration. All glassy-eyed and stuff. It's kind of funny."

"I don't look at his face," Emily says, nor does she look at her own in the mirror above the sink as she spreads toothpaste onto her brush. "I mean when we do it." She leans against the sink and slides sideways toward the wall. "It always reminds me of my dad."

Ramsay is on her knees rummaging through the bottom drawer when Emily says this. She knows enough to stop then and listen to what Emily is saying. She feels herself tighten, ready for what comes next.

"I mean, I never did it with my dad," Emily goes on. Some of the tension leaves Ramsay's shoulders. "He's just the first guy I ever saw have sex."

Ramsay turns around to face Emily. "Well," she says. "This sounds like a story."

"Oh yeah, it's a story all right," Emily says, though she says it with her toothbrush in her mouth so it's hard to understand her exact words. "I don't know what kind, though."

"So tell it. Let's figure it out." Ramsay stretches her legs out in front of her and leans back against the open dresser drawer. Emily finishes brushing, spits twice into the sink before turning back to Ramsay.

"Okay, it was like this." She takes one more deep breath and starts in. "One night my Mom and Dad came home early, earlier than usual. My sister and I were still up. I was about ten years old so that means Annie was about six or so. Anyway, they came in and we weren't in bed yet. We were still watching TV with the baby-sitter. Mom and Dad walk in and my Dad is all bouncy on his feet but my Mom's not saying much. They just walk in and Mom says, 'Time for bed, girls.' And then she says to Rachel, the baby-sitter, that Chet, that's my dad, will take her home.

"So, me and Mom and Annie head upstairs and I decide I want to ride along with my Dad. It wasn't quite bedtime yet, I thought. So I say to my Mom, 'I'm going with Daddy,' and before she can say no I run out to the garage. I wanted to make sure I caught him, you know, so I ran out the front door and came around the driveway. The garage door was shut, which I thought was weird because I didn't think they could've left yet, so I ran around back. The back door had a window." Emily describes a square with her hands as if to set Ramsay right there beside her before she goes on. "So I could see into the garage and I could see right away the car was still in there so I started to open the door. But just when my hand touched the knob," again she holds her hands out, recreating the moment, "I saw Rachel's face. She was stretched out on the hood of the car. I pressed my face up to the glass. I thought something was wrong, you know, like she was sick or something. Then I saw my dad. I still didn't get it. Geez, I was what? Ten years old? How was I supposed to know I wasn't supposed to watch? Well anyway, my dad was really going at it. He looked just like you said. All glassy-eyed and stuff." She shakes her head slowly and looks down at her outstretched hands. "He never saw me, but Rachel Lynn McCormick did. She lay there looking at me and I stood there looking at her. For a long time. She had the bluest eyes I have ever seen on a real person. Then I just went back inside." Emily turns back to the sink and rinses her toothbrush.

"Jesus, Em," Ramsay says. "Jesus."

Emily reaches up and switches off the light above the sink. The desk light haloes the corner of the room.

"Yeah," Emily says. She stretches out on her bed. "I've never told that to anyone before."

"Yeah." Ramsay crawls onto her own bed and curls up. "That's the kind of story it is. A first time story. No matter how many times you tell it, it will always be the first time."

They lie silently for a few minutes. Each wrapped in her own small space.

"So," Ramsay says at last. "What happened then?"

"Oh, you know," Emily answers. "Life went on." She pauses to adjust her pillow. "Did your parents ever fight much?"

"Nah," Ramsay answers. "My family was the prototype for the Nelson family, except they had a girl."

"Your family's not that old," Emily interrupts. "They couldn't be the prototypes because 'proto' means first. I learned that in Greek class just last week."

Ramsay wads up one of the blouses littering her bed and tosses it at Emily.

"You're so smart you make me sick."

"You're just saying that because it's true," Emily answers.

When Emily offered her the gift of her story, Ramsay received it as if it had always been hers, and gave back to Emily, when she named the story, a way to hold on to it and let go of it as well. They could be friends, yes, whatever that means. Whatever that means. Here's the stumbling block: girlfriends, I'm sorry to say, are too often disposable. Whether from nature or from nurture, they're the people we spend time with between the real moments, the real relationships of our lives. When the time comes the friendship dies a seemingly natural death. Fewer shared secrets, more days, weeks, months between conversations. But that didn't happen to these two. From the opening dance of shared secrets they both knew they could trust one another. They could be friends, whatever that meant.

They shared a decade, a third of a lifetime for Ramsay. Ten seasons of lilacs blooming and dying again. Sometimes they stopped to enjoy their show, sometimes not. This conversation, one of their last, the one Emily will replay and replay and replay, is not enough, but it is all there is.

"Okay," Ramsay calls from the bedroom. "I have six more outfits for you to look at."

"Six? You bought six more outfits?" Emily looks up from the crossword puzzle she is working on in the corner of Ramsay's cluttered kitchen table.

"Well yeah, but not really." Ramsay is immediately flustered in the way she gets only before going home. "See, five of them are going back. I mean it's not like I've gone completely off the deep end."

"If you say so," Emily says skeptically.

"Em, help me out here," Ramsay says. She carries two full-length mirrors into the room and props them up, one in front of the sink the other in front of the stove. "Like it's not bad enough that my brother's getting married to my ex-best friend, I have to go and act like it's no big deal that they didn't ask me to be in the wedding. Because it isn't, but everybody else thinks it is and so I have to go back to my hometown and waltz through family and friends with just the right amount of . . . of . . . je ne sais quoi . . ."

"Ooh, you're speaking French," Emily cuts in. "This is really serious."

"Just the right something," Ramsay goes on, adjusting the mirrors and talking as much to her own images as to Emily, "so that those people can see I'm okay about all this. That I'm okay about the marriage. That I'm okay about not being married. That I'm . . . that I'm okay." She picks up several of the bags off the table and begins to talk louder over the crinkling of paper and plastic. "Because I am okay. I know I don't sound okay right this minute and I can just hear them thinking, 'Methinks she doth protest too much,' though of course none of them would actually quote Shakespeare, but I am. Okay I mean." She disappears into the bedroom and her voice is alternately muffled and loud as she tries the first of the six outfits on. "I like my life. I like my job. I like doing what I do and I know that my family thinks something is wrong, terribly wrong with me because I'm not doing what they think I should be doing – family, kids, blah blah blah. They just can't seem to adjust to the idea that I'm not the little girl from Minot anymore and that I actually grew up and became someone they don't really know or, in some cases, like Lisa's, my soon to be sister-in-law, someone they don't care to know. I mean, people change. Is that such an unbelievable concept?" With that last question Ramsay steps suddenly back into the room, clutching a jacket to her chest as if beseeching Emily for wisdom or divine grace.

Emily looks up from her crossword again and stares at Ramsay's face for a moment.

"What's a six-letter word for 'supply with dikes'?" she asks.

Ramsay's forehead furrows and unfurrows, then she starts to laugh. Slow at first, then hard enough that she has to lean against the door. Emily bursts out laughing then, too. At everything. At nothing.

There it is. Can you hear it? See it? That connection between them? It's there. What is it? What is it? If you could name it, take it out and look at it, talk about it, you could make it stronger, make it last. I know you could. Why are there no words for this?

Instead, they go on with the style show, through the six outfits but not to a decision. In the end Ramsay lays each of the outfits on her bed and she and Emily bring kitchen chairs into the room to sit and watch the clothes. They drink red wine from thrift store crystal and just look at each of the outfits. They knew how to be silent together.

"Oh, I've been wanting to tell you about the dream I had last night," Ramsay says at last. Not to fill the silence, but to share something she couldn't identify with Emily. "In the dream there had been this cave-in of some sort and I was digging bodies out of the sand. The sand was really fine, not gritty like normal sand, so I could pull bodies out easily. But I wasn't in any big hurry." She sips her wine and goes on. "I mean I knew there was a bunch of bodies beneath the sand I was on but I just slowly pulled up one body and blew the sand away from its face and then leisurely pulled out another. The bodies were really hot, like feverish, but dry and not breathing. The really weird thing about it was that all the bodies were me." Emily looks up at her then and watches her face. "In the dream I didn't think it was weird, but when I woke up this morning I couldn't stop thinking about it. It probably means something really deep, but I don't know what."

"You get so weird whenever you get ready to go home," Emily says.

"I know," Ramsay nods. "Psycho daughter."

"Well, no, I don't mean psycho." She shrugs. "Just nervous."

Ramsay drinks the last of her wine and reaches for the bottle at her feet. "I know. It's just that when I'm here everything makes sense. But back home they've got these rules about how everyone should act, how everyone should be. I can't convince anyone up there about even the smallest things. Like remember the deal with Lisa – how when we used to be friends she would always cancel our plans if a boy asked her out. I hated that, but whenever I got mad I'd get lectured at by everyone from my mom to the minister that –"

"The minister?" Emily cuts in.

"Yeah, my uncle. Anyway, they all said I would understand when I fell in love and blah, blah, blah, but I have fallen in love, more than once, and I still think you're supposed to be able to trust your friends. But none of them saw it that way."

"Do you still try to convince them?"

"No. I gave that up after college, when I really moved away. When I got down here I told myself it was live and let live. When I'm here that philosophy works just fine, but..." Her voice trails off.

"But, you're afraid they'll convince you?" Emily asks.

Ramsay thinks for a moment before answering. "Yeah," she says. "I'm afraid I'm not as strong as I think I am."

Emily pours the last of the wine into her class then thrusts her glass up imperatively into the silence that followed Ramsay's words, "You," she says, "are as strong as you need to be. You will wear that power suit over there and you will be stunningly beautiful and independent and what they don't understand will be no concern of ours. When you get back, we'll drink shots of tequila until the provincial poison of the north is cleansed from your blood. When we're done with that we'll dig through the sand together and decide which one of those selves is even worth worrying about. As for the others, we'll give them a proper burial." They clink their glasses in a toast. "While you're gone, I'll have the same dream. We'll be a couple of Born Agains."

"Ooh, woman, I like it when you go off on your pep talk tangents," Ramsay says. "I feel better already. Does your name fit into the boxes of the 'supply with dikes' clue?" Emily picks the puzzle off the floor and checks. "Only if I spell it wrong."

"Maybe we should consider new names, too."

"When you come back, ma Cherie. When you come back."

They both laugh then. Not the wild giggle of before, but the comfortable laugh one has when life feels good. Emily looks at Ramsay for a lingering moment, at the way her brown hair cascades off her shoulder when she turns her head, at her straight, patrician nose that gives her face the chiseled look of a classic beauty. She looks at her with love, but she says, "Well, let's get back to our job of keeping you out of debtors' prison and make a decision. I say power suit, all the way." She picks up a gray silk suit jacket and holds it up. The moment to tell one another they love one another, that their lives are richer for having shared it, passes. And it doesn't, as we already know, come again.

To say that Emily thinks constantly of Ramsay's death would not be completely true. One does not think about breathing or the heart beating. In that way, Emily does not think about Ramsay's death, though it is always with her.

The pain of loss has been written and rewritten and yet no words plumb the depth of that abyss. Language, always an opaque medium, is rendered even more so in the service of grief. No way to talk about this thing, this hole she feels spreading, deepening, swallowing her. That's what she thinks of now, of the incomprehensible extent of the emptiness that is now her life.

She walks east from her office in the administration building not seeing the purple crocuses, the appearance of which she has noted and relayed to Ramsay every spring for eight years. Her car, which she left on the north side of 'R' Street in front of the Historical Society, seems too far away for her tiredness.

She walks almost to 16th Street before she realizes she has passed her car and she turns back west, stopping for a moment to stare at a crack in the side walk, a Doublemint gum wrapper, a cigarette butt at her feet. Then she looks up to regain her bearings, walks toward her car.

Having missed it the first time she doesn't believe what her eyes do not see. She keeps walking, almost as far as the Union, before stopping to look up and down the street, searching for the blue Sentra.

Her first reaction is to widen the scope of her search. Scanning both sides of the street she replays her trip downtown, watching herself on the mental screen as she recalls turning off 17th Street, slowing for a pack of bicyclists, almost missing the gift of this parking space. A car, no, a pick-up, was just starting to back out when she reached it. She knows that despite all her loss, she still has the capacity to remember where she parked.

She walks to the space, third in a line of six meters between the Historical Society and the Student Union. She stands staring at the black Trans Am in her place.

The thoughts come slowly at first, possible explanations for the car's absence, but when the truth comes it erupts inside of her, volcanic, forcing the name from her mouth.

"Ramsay." She says it more as a statement than a question. "Ramsay took my car," she says to the parking meter, the third in a line of six, testing the truth of it on her tongue. Ramsay is the only other person who had a key. It had to be Ramsay. It would be so like her to borrow the car, thinking she would get it back in time to surprise Emily with her own car and the fact of Ramsay's presence. It would be so like Ramsay to get mixed up in some ghoulishly bizarre mistake like this that made everyone believe she was dead, but in truth she was just late, missed her bus, her plane, her own death.

It has happened, you know. Cases of mistaken identity that result in delayed tragedy for one, resurrection for another. Remember the car accident not long ago? Two boys so badly burned as to be unrecognizable – one dead, one alive. The doctors made the wrong identification. The family and friends of the living boy believed they were the ones who had lost a loved one. It was a month, an entire month before the living boy could speak, before he could tell them of their mistake. He was alive. They had carved the wrong name on the tombstone.

It has happened other times, too. A stolen purse, a fatal accident. It can happen. It has happened. It did happen,

Emily thinks. She claps her hand to her mouth to catch the peal of laughter. Of course, this would happen to Ramsay. Emily could hear her now.

"It was just so bee-zarre to see my own obituary." She would be breathless, as if she were letting you in on the middle of a conversation. "I mean, on the one hand I felt sort of like Tom Sawyer, you know, when he sneaks in on his own funeral – or was that Huck Finn? I can never remember – anyway, I couldn't just call you and say, 'Oh, by the way, Em, I'm not dead.' It would be just too weird so I flew home so I could tell you in person."

I can't wait to hear her explanation for why stealing my car would make that whole conversation easier, Emily thinks. Oh Ramsay, Ramsay! Her name something between a song and a prayer. Ramsay.

Emily runs up the steps of the Union, runs though she wants to skip, yes, skip, like a little girl, like joy itself. At the phone in the hallway she dials the first five digits of Ramsay's number before she remembers she needs to deposit a quarter. "Idiot," she mutters. Trembling fingers push the coin into the slot. She listens to the maddening slowness of the technology. She hears the first ring, second, third, and at last the redemptive click of connection.

"Ramsay!" Emily shouts. And Ramsay answers her.

"If you're calling to tell me I'm late, I already know. Tell it to my machine." Then the series of seven short beeps and one long, followed by the alert silence of a machine waiting.

Into that silence creeps Emily's first doubt. Unlike the eruption of her resurrection, the returned certainty of Ramsay's death seeps into the fiber of Emily, becomes her.

She presses her forehead hard against the partition between the phones. No, she does not want to know this. She wants to know Ramsay is in her car right now, looking for Emily. See how tightly she holds herself, resisting truth, resisting death.

I don't know how long she stands there. Long enough for Ramsay's machine to click off, for the dial tone to return. She

refuses to think of the alternate possibilities, other explanations for her car's absence. Still, she is no longer able to picture Ramsay behind the wheel, no longer able to hear her
voice explaining away the awkwardness of her actions. Soon
though, she will hang up the phone, stand straighter, and
walk out of the Union. Because that's what we do. Grief does
not kill us, a fact that seems unjust in the face of the pain it
brings us. Emily will wipe her face, brush back her hair, and
walk out of the Union. She will decide to not call the police,
not report the missing car, at least not yet. She will go home.
She will find no sympathy cards in her mailbox; even card
companies have missed this market.

Yes, it will settle, this tempest of her grief. It will become
the hollow ache she becomes aware of during the so-called
epiphanies of life: marriage, childbirth, loss. But it will be in
the small unremarkable moments of life that Emily's grief will
return to her. When the crocuses come late one spring, or an
old recipe flutters loose from a cookbook, she will stumble
upon this grief, this diamond, and it will be as hard, as bril-
liant, as precious as it was the day she first knew it.

ASHES TO ASHES

In death, the skin of my grandmother's face lies smooth and clear. The skeletal clarity of her head upon the satin pillow recalls the young girl who once penned on the back of a postcard to her sister, "Love Conquers All." That postcard, found some ten years back pressed between the yellowed pages of one of her books, may have been the one thing that kept me from hating this woman of my own blood.

Behind me, my grandfather accepts the condolences of neighbors and friends. Turning my head toward him I can see his stiff back, his slightly bowed head. I watch the line of blue-haired women creak toward him. I see the way their hands shake as they reach out to take his hand, touch his shoulder, and I am struck by the graciousness with which he receives their sympathy and good wishes. His tall frame has always seemed so awkward in crowds. Now he seems to know just what's expected of him, as if his recent widowerhood has freed him to be someone new, someone self-assured, admirable.

At the sight, I feel the bitter bile of resentment rise in the back of my throat and I turn away from this apparition. Across the room I see my sister, Beck, trapped between a massive spray of gladiolus and one of Grandma's former neighbors. Everyone around me is speaking in the hushed tones appropriate to this solemn occasion, everyone except Beck. She is shouting into the ear of the old woman.

"No, I'm not Mary. I'm Rebecca, Phinn's youngest."

I have to laugh to myself because she sounds like a broken record. It seems Beck and I grew up invisible. Everyone in this town remembers our older sister, but on us they draw a blank. I first became aware of this phenomenon when my mother took Beck and me along to a PTA meeting when Mary was in the eighth grade. We were four and six, cute enough ages, but the teachers who stopped to talk to Mom talked about Mary, about her intelligence, her charm, her beauty. I still remember one woman saying, "Sometimes in class I can hardly take my eyes off Mary. She is just so striking."

Mom nodded, I suppose in agreement. Then the woman cast her eyes down toward Beck and me. I expected her to comment on us somehow, but apparently she was still blinded by Mary's beauty. Even Beck's stage whisper to me, "I just let a stinker," brought no response. She neither saw us nor smelled us before Mom rushed us toward the next of Mary's admirers.

Before I have a chance to rescue Beck from the deaf woman, my cousin, Cam, appears at my side. She places her hand in the small of my back and whispers softly, "How are you holding up, Rachel?"

She married a minister and sometimes I have trouble telling them apart. This is the third time in two hours that she's asked me this question. She's decent enough, but I always get the feeling when I talk to her that it's not really her there talking to me. Everything she says seems prerecorded.

"Fine," I say, looking over the top of her head toward the casket. "Better than Grandma."

Just as I expected, my response is deemed inappropriate. She turns on her heel and walks away, her red hair its own reprimand.

Cam looks like her father, red hair, pale complexion and poor eyesight. She is soft-spoken, blushes easily and rarely looks a person in the eye. Despite the shiftiness implied by that trait she seems to have dedicated her life to trying to do the right thing. Unfortunately the right thing doesn't include a sense of humor. I'm not sure if that's the result or the cause of having married a minister.

When we were young, when we were friends, that statement would have made her laugh. Now she doesn't laugh, but she will forgive, and that will make her feel even better than the joke should have.

After the funeral dinner in the basement of the KC hall, when everyone has had enough of the casseroles, Jell-O salads, and death talk, they begin to meander in groups toward the exit door. Cam again appears at my shoulder and tells me she is taking Grandpa out to see the farm.

"Is this your idea or his?" I ask. The top of her head is level with the plane of my shoulder and though I try not to I find myself feeling as if I am talking to a child.

"I guess he suggested it," she says somewhat defensively. "He said he hadn't been out there since Grandma got sick. He seemed to want to go."

I nod. I don't tell her it's a damn fool idea. In our family we don't say that sort of thing. We may tell one another we think the other has bought the wrong house, got the wrong hair cut, married the wrong person, but the important stuff we just let slide.

"Been out there lately?" I ask. She must detect a note of criticism in my voice because before she answers blotches of red spread slowly up her neck and onto her cheeks.

"Well, no," she replies. "But I talked to the neighbor. He's been keeping an eye on things."

Again I nod and say nothing.

When we were younger Beck and I didn't pay much attention to Cam. We moved in each other's orbits only as much as family gatherings demanded, holidays and the like. Our dad and Cam's mother – brother and sister – talked to one another if they had to, but only if they had to. I could never piece together any sort of story about how or why they didn't get along. They just didn't and that was that. The way it has always been.

Sometime in our teens, before her parents moved their family up to Montana, circumstances threw us together and we spent some time in each other's company. I think it was around the time we discovered both alcohol and God. I remember lying in bed long after my parents had gone to sleep, sharing a bottle of cheap wine and whispering excerpts from Revelations to one another. It was the kind of friendship that slips in close to your heart, almost unnoticed. Like most experiences one has in youth, it became a model for friendships later in life. For better or for worse, real life experience never matches the memory. When we got older one of us kept the alcohol, the other kept the god and so we grew apart. Though Cam and I still write at Christmas and send cards on birthdays we no longer find much to talk about. As a result, I don't know now what to tell her about what the neighbor was keeping an eye on. In the cold January sunshine I let her take my grandfather's arm and walk him to her car.

From the front seat of my own car I watch the two of them walk away. My grandfather, at this point in time, is still close to six feet tall. Shoulders only slightly stooped, he carries himself, for reasons unclear to me, proudly. He allows Cam to open the car door for him, lets her tuck a blanket across his lap and stares straight ahead until she closes the door and goes around to the driver's side.

As they pull away from the curb, Beck crawls into the car beside me. She does this by putting her head in first, placing a hand out and leaning forward as she sticks in her foot. After that she brings in the bulk of her body and last of all her right leg. My Japanese-make car shifts noticeably as she settles in. The door catches tufts of brown grass as she pulls it shut.

"The French have a word for that," I say. "A word for the curb-swelling phenomenon."

"Oh yeah?" Beck answers. She tugs on her skirt once

before giving up, then fishes a cigarette out of her purse. "Phenomenon you say? You college girls are so smart. What's French for fuck you?"

We both laugh. Because we love each other best we insult each other most. I open both windows because I hate the smell of cigarette smoke.

"Did Cam tell you she was taking Grandpa out to the farm?" I ask as I maneuver my car into the lane of slow-moving traffic.

"You're shittin' me." Her eyes widen and her hand stops midway to her mouth, the flame of her lighter flickering in the blast from the heater and the breeze from the open windows.

"Nope. Apparently Grandfather Vincent expressed an interest in seeing 'the farm'."

"Shit," she says, taking a long slow drag on her cigarette. "Shit. Shit."

The farm, as we so fondly refer to it, is a cluster of buildings at the edge of somebody else's cornfield. There used to be a barn where my grandparents milked cows, raised calves and stored all the tools and machines a farmer needs to do those sorts of things. A hard Nebraska wind took it to the ground one day and a few years later a bulldozer destroyed the evidence of its existence.

To the north of that there used to be a hog barn, but that was one of the first buildings sacrificed to progress when the land was leased out and converted to crop use. My grandfather learned years ago how to make money with the least amount of work. The hog barn exists only in the memory of the oldest family members. Mary remembers falling into the sow pen and being saved from certain death by my angry and frightened father. Her eyes still get wide telling about how mad Dad was that day. The moral of that family story was supposed to be that there is nothing more dangerous than a mother protecting her young, but what I got out of it was don't do anything stupid in front of my dad and if anything stupid happens to you, don't let him know. To my knowledge the hog barn doesn't even show up in pictures.

A cool, gray day in late October was the last time I had been out to that place. I was moving out of the college dorm and moving into an unfurnished apartment with two friends from school. Mom mentioned that there might be a few things worth saving still in the house. Nothing she wanted, but we girls might find something if we cared to look.

Mary and my two brothers are several years older than Beck and me so most hand-me-down heirlooms had been picked over years before. Still, I'm an optimist if I'm anything at all so after breakfast one Saturday, Beck and I borrowed brother Bill's beat-up old pickup and headed out for a day of scavenging.

"Let's just avoid any ugly bickering," I told Beck before we set out. "I'll drive and I'll pay for the gas, but I get Grandma's oak rocker if it's still there."

"Yeah, right," she snorted then switched to a Southern Belle accent. "Why Rachel Lynn, I would just love to help you haul everything down the steps and out of the house. I'll even help you load it into the pickup, just to make sure you get all the good stuff."

"Well, 'good stuff' may be stretching it, given that Mary's been out there more than once since Vince and June moved out, but you get the idea. 'Me first,' is my motto for the day." I punched a few buttons on the radio to see if Bill had gotten it fixed yet. "Hell, you're married. You had what, six showers, and everybody who is anybody was at your wedding bearing gifts. You don't need anything."

"Two," she said. "I had two showers. I don't want the rocker, but I'm not forfeiting my dibbing rights to anything before we see it." She dug a cigarette out of her purse and smoked half of it before going on. "Like getting married means you don't need anything. Get a clue, Sally Rogers."

I looked over to see if she had more to say. She didn't.

"Why little Laura Petrie, I can't imagine that you and Rob are anything but two love birds. Why soon you'll be announcing the arrival of a darling little Ritchie and your lives will be complete."

This is an ongoing joke between us, comparing our lives to the old sitcoms. Of course we don't measure up, nobody ever does, but we hadn't thought of that yet.

"No." Her tone turned oddly serious. "I think I'll pass on little Ritchie. I don't see any reason to bring another kid into this world just to screw him up."

Beck stopped talking then and the lack of a radio in the old pickup became more of a problem. Nothing to take our minds off the words she left hanging between us. The hum of the tires on the highway changed to a high-pitched whine when we reached the new part just outside of town and it gave the cab of the pickup the air of a caffeine rush or a bad dream screaming around the back of my head.

When we were little, I used to think Beck was My Job. I was in charge of seeing that she got her hands washed before meals, that she got out of bed before she started peeing, that she didn't bother anybody. When I was seven or eight I had this nightmare where there was a virus in the house – I had just found out that a virus was some kind of bug – and the virus got into people's eyes and ate their eyeballs in half. I remember how everybody in the family except Beck and me went blind. They were walking around with these mealy white blobs where their eyes used to be. In the dream I told Beck she had to keep her eyes closed tight so the bug wouldn't get in.

"Squeeze 'em as tight as you can," I told her. In the dream we sat on our bed, trying to stay away from those blind strangers who had once been our family. I remember how scared I felt in the dream. I was the only one who could pro-tect Beck and so I sat holding her, rocking her, saying, "Keep squeezing, I won't let the bug get you." Over and over I said it until Beck's quiet whimpering turned to sobs and she turned her face toward me. When she opened her eyes I saw the bug had gotten her too. I woke up screaming.

About thirty minutes into the trip, during which time we hadn't said much of anything, I looked over at Beck and said, "You know, it's pretty chilly today." I didn't think I would need to explain what I meant.

She looked back at me for just a second.

"Yeah, probably need something to warm us up."

I passed the corner where we need to turn north to the farm and kept going toward Prague.

"We'll just see if Sam's Liquor Store is open."

"If it is, we'll know God wants us to have a drink even though it isn't quite noon," Beck said. "Cam's always telling me to look for signs of God's word."

At that point, even before we tipped back a swig of schnapps, we started getting giddy, making stupid jokes and laughing at everything. Beck's one of those people who can always make me laugh. Not just because she says funny things, but because she makes me feel my jokes are funny, too. Sometimes we get to laughing so hard about nothing that I truly fear I'll die laughing. I mean, just when I think I've calmed down enough to where I can catch a gasp of air, I'll hear that tiny squeak Beck makes when she is laughing and can't breathe either. We're even worse when we've had a drink or three. It just stands to reason that by the time we reached the farm we had a regular party going on. I remember how much we laughed that day because of what happened when we stopped laughing.

I almost missed the driveway, only partly because of the alcohol. Weeds had taken over the yard and the plum thicket seemed to have spread out to more than twice its former size. From the front the house looked pretty much the same: lonely and abandoned, the way old unlived-in farm houses do, but it had started looking that way before the grandparents had moved into town. The white clapboard siding needed painting then and it needed it now. Grandpa wasn't much of a fix-it man and Grandma was sick more often than not for as long as I can remember. Whenever Beck and I stayed out there she mostly ignored us, staying in her room with the shades pulled and the

TV on. Sometimes, when I got older and no longer stayed out there, I let myself think that if just once she'd gotten up and looked after us – we were just little girls for God's sake – things would have been different. But she didn't, and they weren't.

From the back though, where the driveway led us, the house looked rougher. Two panes on an upstairs window were missing and the end post on the back porch had slipped off its foundation so the roof drooped down, giving the whole house the appearance of a stroke victim.

"Wow," Beck said as we sat and stared from inside the heated pickup. For a minute I thought she was going to cry. We passed the bottle back and forth between us one more time. "I didn't know it would be like this," she said.

We sat in the pickup, the heater blasting, staring at the memories. The longer we sat the more of them came flooding back. My cheeks felt flushed and my heart didn't exactly start pounding, but I did feel each individual beat.

"Well," I said, finally, shutting off the engine. "Let's go see what we can see."

Following my lead, Beck opened her door.

"Take what we can take," she replied.

And so we did.

When my grandparents moved into town, my grandfather said he was moving only because of Grandma.

"I could stay," he told my mother, his daughter-in-law, "but she won't. She seems to think we need help."

This he said sitting beside the heat stove while my mother fixed them supper, something she did nightly for three years. The senior center only delivered lunch.

When we moved them into the nursing home he said he only did it for her. "I'm strong enough to live alone."

My grandmother – what did she say all this time? Nothing that I can remember. She did not leave me with any words of advice or wisdom.

Once on one holiday or another, just before she died, she arrived in a wheel chair. My brothers carried her and her chair up the steps. Like a queen she held her head straight and trusted them to get her into the warmth of the kitchen.

After dinner, when she needed a nap like the smallest of children, we found that her chair would not fit through the bedroom door. Beck and I said we could help her through the door to the bed. Only three or four steps. Easy.

I remember reaching under her arm and grasping, my fingers almost completely encircling it, and being shocked by how much smaller she was than I remembered her. Bird-like bone in my hand, I pulled upward as she pushed with her legs and lunged forward.

We all thought her legs would hold her so we were caught off guard when she dropped almost to the floor. Only the closeness of the bed saved her. She lay partially on the bed and what I remember most clearly about that moment was the tear that squeezed out the corner of her eye, crept down the side of her long, curved nose.

"Leave me alone," she said. "Leave. Me. Alone."

We closed the door on a ninety year-old body curled into the fetal position.

She tried to keep cooking, right up to the end. All of her pans were scorched and the curtains by the kitchen stove had black streaks on them from the day my mother didn't get there in time.

My grandfather never learned to cook. But still, he always believed he could care for himself. That belief is what propelled him out the door of the parish hall into my cousin's car and down the road to the end of his life.

Cam really believed she was giving him the chance to say goodbye. She never knew about his plan to move back to the farm after Grandma's death. She never knew about the grocery sack in the back of his closet where he kept a change of clothes, his pajamas, and some chewing tobacco, in preparation for the day when he could sneak out the side door of the nursing home, slide behind the wheel of the beat-up Chevrolet he still had parked in the back lot, and head out to the farm to end his days, as he had said on more than one occasion, "in peace." I never understood how he could believe that about peace, but that's what he said.

At his funeral, just three months after we buried Grandma, Cam stands weeping beside an inevitable spray of gladiolus. Although I don't want to go to her, I loom on the horizon of her peripheral vision and she turns toward me with red swollen eyes.

"It's so hard to believe they're both gone," she says.

I stand there dumbly looking down on her pale face and wonder what she thinks, what she remembers. I know she was once like me. In the spell of that cheap wine and discovery of holy words we found a way to trust one another. I said to her what I had said, aloud, to no one. Not even Beck. Her soft voice had revealed the same past.

But somewhere along the line she had left it all behind. Standing here now I think about that nightmare from my childhood and I feel a shrill of fear.

"They are, though," I say quietly. She looks at me a long time before going on.

"I remember how much I used to admire your stoicism. You seem so calm in the face of all tragedies."

"Well," I answer, "not all." When I swallow, I think the sound must echo in the sanctuary, but Cam doesn't seem to notice.

If I were making this story up, this would be the moment we would turn to one another, take off our life masks, and just hold one another tight. "He's gone now," we would say. "We're safe." And we would cry there in one another's arms, for as long as we need to. Or forever, whichever came first.

But I'm not making this up, so instead Cam says, "He looks good, doesn't he?"

I look at the flowers behind her, at the cross above her head where an agonized Christ hangs in perpetuity. I suck my teeth a little bit and then say, "Yeah, just like himself."

Beck's hand touches the crook of my arm and I turn to

her so quickly she takes a step back.

"Relax," she says. "It's just me."

The three of us stand there in a silence that lasts long enough for it to become awkward.

"He must have really loved her, huh?" Cam says, looking toward the casket.

"What?" I snort, though I try not to.

"I don't know, he just never seemed to pull himself together after she died. It was like grief killed him or something." Cam's tears start sliding down her cheeks again. "I'll never forget how sad he was the day of Grandma's funeral. It was so terrible to see what vandals had done to that house. It was just a crime. A crime and a sin."

Beck and I look at one another.

"Yeah," I say. "A crime."

"And a sin," Beck says. For a surreal moment I think Beck and I are going to start laughing, the inappropriate, uncontrollable kind we are known for, but instead we just look at one another. Beck's eyes are deep blue, like mine, no sign of blindness there and I know I'm not alone.

For the rest of the funeral I stay at the back of the church. I never see what death does to the surprised and saddened expression Grandpa has worn since the day we buried Grandma. Around me I hear people echoing Cam's belief that he lost his will to live when his wife died. But I know it wasn't grief. I know it was something that began and ended the day he found the broken windows, the raccoon shit smeared on the walls of his little castle and, most of all, the blackened circle outside his old bedroom window where the charred remains of his bed lay in clear view of anyone who cared to look that way.

As the pallbearers carry out the casket, I stay standing by the door accepting condolences from vaguely familiar faces. To most I just smile a trifle sadly and say thanks. But to one old woman squeezing my hand, I try something on for size.

"Good riddance," I say.

She smiles, hearing only what I should say, and replies, "I know, dear. I know."

ORPHANS

F ive months, two weeks, and four days ago, an early morning vandalism spree resulted in bullet holes through the plate glass windows of seven of the twenty-four businesses on Main Street, the stained glass windows of four churches (two Catholic, one Lutheran, and one Methodist), and miscellaneous windows of four residences. The spree culminated in the death of my wife, who was standing precisely in the middle of our living room at approximately 3:30 a.m.

Theories abound as to who's responsible for the vandalism-turned-murder. For several weeks two high school students were considered the likeliest suspects. The Owens' boy and his sidekick, the youngest of the Johnson clan, have been getting in trouble with the law since shortly after they got a merit badge in carpentry and discovered their dads' chain saws worked as well on those old wooden light posts as they did on a two-by-four. The last time they came through the court system was for a spree of mailbox baseball. They left a trail of dented and dislocated mailboxes all over the county. They had never hurt anybody, but they damaged things with impunity.

Only once have they been known to use a gun on their rampages. That just last year when they played duck shoot with the trophy window at the high school. The Murphy Bros. Carnival Show had just been through on its annual stop and kids all over town were playing their own version of the game booths in their backyards. Owen and Johnson were always a little too creative.

Police Chief Fox dismissed them as suspects, though, after he verified that on the night in question, the night my wife was killed, they were in jail up on a South Dakota Indian reservation. It seems they tried to carry their games too far.

Joe Roskins, who lives with his wife in a doublewide three miles north of town, became the next suspect. Three weeks after my wife died Joe blasted holes through the side of Jim Peters' barn. He and Jim Peters have been fighting since they got out of high school twenty years ago. I'm not sure what started it all. Most think a woman was at the heart of it, but no one knows for sure.

Both of them are the genial sort. Joe once got up at 2 a.m. on a windy January night and fired up his John Deere to pull my car out of a snowdrift. A midnight madness run Carole and I used to take when the kids were in their teens had ended unceremoniously on an unplowed section road about a mile from Joe's house. I had walked to Joe's house, woke him and his wife and asked if I could use his phone to call for a ride.

"What about your car?" he had asked, rubbing the heel of his hand into his eye.

"I'll call a tow truck in the morning and we can take care of it in daylight," I answered.

He stood in the doorway looking over my shoulder for a minute, then muttered, "Fuck that." In a louder voice he added, "Come on in while I get some clothes on."

His John Deere had a cab, but no heater and our frosty breath hung in the silence between us. The only time he spoke was to ask if Peters still owned the only tow truck in town. When we got to the car Carole got out and came toward us, wrapping her coat around her.

"Mike, I thought you were going to call for one of the boys to come get us! Joe, you didn't have to get up. Mike, we could take care of this tomorrow." Her face muscles showed the struggle of frowning at one person and smiling at another at the same time.

"It's okay, ma'am," Joe said and dropped down on his back in the snow and crawled under the rear of the Oldsmobile to hook the towrope onto the axle.

"One of us could have done that, Joe," Carole said, looking at me. We both knew who that one should be. I shrugged at her.

I tried to give Joe some money for his trouble, but he wouldn't hear of it.

That was eight years ago. When Chief Fox called and told me about how Joe shot up Peters' barn and he thought he would bring him in for questioning about my wife's case, I couldn't help but feel the Chief was getting desperate for leads.

"Joe and Jim have been going eye for an eye after each other for more than twenty years," I said. "You know he wouldn't come in and shoot up the whole town. Even if he got drunk."

"People do strange things sometimes," Fox said. "I hear from my dispatcher that Joe's wife is fixin' to leave him."

I still didn't think Joe was crazy enough to shoot out windows in houses where people were living, but Fox knew his job better than I did. I'd been prosecuting his cases long enough to know that.

As it turned out, Joe's wife wasn't planning on leaving him at all. She'd been traveling to Omaha to see a specialist for more than a year. Seems she and Joe wanted to have a baby together and they were doing anything they could to make one. They were home in bed together that night.

It's been four months since Fox has had a suspect even that good. About two months ago he stopped returning my calls the same day I made them, but last week he called me without being asked.

"Look, Mike, I'm not saying I'm closing the case," he said,

without bothering with a hello. "I want you to know we'll keep trying. But hell, you and I both know how these things go. We have three people who think they saw the vehicle. One swears it was a late model pickup, the other two agree that it was a car, but hell they can't get together on the size, the color, or the make." I could hear him tapping his pen to his teeth at the other end of the line, a habit he had developed a few years ago when his doctor made him give up smoking. "All I got are bullets. From a .22 for Christ's sake. Hell, kids start getting their first gun before they're ten years old around here. And ninety percent of them are .22s." He paused for a long time, but I waited to let him finish. "I'm doin' my best, Mike. You know?"

From my office window, I could look across the square and see the repaired windows of the donut shop and the dress shop. Though hidden from me now by the bulk of the court-house in the center of the square, I knew all the windows of all the businesses had been repaired. Even the churches had replaced windows or repaired the tiny holes. No signs left.

We're what's considered a bedroom community. Forty-nine percent of the people who live in this town work in the city. When I was young, it was a rare man who drove east at dawn to the city, but now a steady stream of headlights pours out of town when the sun comes up. Those who stay put complain about the drain, cuss the commuters for coming home with their back seats loaded with groceries and their tanks filled with gas. Still, most of us realize the advantages of having them on the tax rolls and when things get slow or go bad, more of us join them.

I think that time may have come for me now. I know it must have been someone just passing through on a joy ride who shot up the town. Kids from the city, most likely. I can't get over the feeling that we're all just sitting ducks here, that the city's steam-rolling through this town.

Carole and I grew up here. She was homecoming queen of 1966, the same year the Cougars missed the class B state football championship title by one failed field goal attempt in the last fifty-six seconds of the game.

I didn't see that last play. I sat silently in the stands watching Carole's face as she and the other cheerleaders pleaded with God and screamed with passion at the players, and the spectators, and the football itself to please go over that goal post. Her face contorted and she dropped to her knees and I knew we had lost the game.

I remember I stood up on my seat to watch her move with the sea of people toward the players on the field. I watched her throw her arms around Ken Jackson's neck and at that moment I thought no other quarterback in history could win more.

I was a junior at the university before I found the courage to talk to her. We ended up in a History of the Roman Empire class together. Though she moved in a phalanx of girlfriends most of the time I managed to get a seat beside her on the day our seat assignments were set.

What I have always considered our first date was for her nothing more than a free ride home for the weekend. I bought her french fries and a cherry coke at the Dairy Queen on the edge of town so I said it was officially a date. She always said our first date was a double with my roommate, Steve, and her best friend, Maggie.

"We went to a movie. On 'O' Street," she said, as if remembering the place was the proof I needed that she loved me from the start. She may have loved me then, I would reply, but that wasn't the start.

"You were a daffodil in the spring pageant the year you were in third grade and I was in fourth," I said. "I was a frog. I was squatting on the floor beside you when you 'bloomed' and three of your petals came loose and dangled around your hips. Your chin quivered the whole show, but you didn't cry. That was the start."

The big brick building where we attended school is boarded up and surrounded by an eight-foot high chain-link fence. Our kids went to school with kids from a three-county area in a massive, spreading complex at the edge of town.

The gas station where I got my first after-school job is now a parking lot for an absentee-owned apartment complex.

These sorts of changes weigh on me, and once before I thought we would leave it all behind. Go somewhere where even the old stuff was new to us. A law firm in Kansas City offered me a job as trial lawyer the year Annie started third grade. Steve, my old college roommate and current senior partner in the firm, sent me a bottle of twelve year-old scotch to celebrate the offer.

The offer process took several weeks from the time Steve first tossed the idea out with his racquetball serve to the day the scotch showed up special delivery at our front door. The day I told Carole about the idea her only comment was, "Sounds like something Steve would do." I thought she meant Steve was the kind of guy who didn't forget about his friends.

The day the scotch arrived I wanted to open it right away and celebrate, even though it was only 10:00 a.m., but Carole said she thought we ought to wait. We didn't drink much then and certainly not so early in the day, so I agreed to wait.

I remember I asked Annie what she thought about living in the city. I asked the boys if they thought they would like to join a soccer league. I danced Annie around the kitchen. I chased the boys up and down the stairs until Carole screamed, "Enough." Then I grabbed Carole and kissed her neck and told her I would buy her a beautiful, diamond necklace for her beautiful noble neck.

"Don't bother," she said. She pushed away from me and took out a watering can from beneath the sink. "We aren't moving."

"What?" I wasn't quite sure I had heard her right.

"I have no intention of moving me or the children to Kansas City, or anywhere else for that matter," she said. With her back still toward me, she climbed onto a step stool and began watering her plants. "Of course, you can do what you want."

"But I thought you wanted to. I thought . . . "

"No, you didn't, Michael." She turned toward me. With

her face framed by the leaves of a fern hanging low in the skylight she reminded me of the little girl-daffodil I fell in love with. "You never thought anything. You just wanted something and you went after it. You didn't think about what I wanted. You never do."

I was standing right in front of her and God I wanted to hit her. I wanted to strike her beautiful face. I thought about how I just wanted to make her happy. All my life I had been trying to make her happy. If I was successful in my job, I just knew she would be happy. This is what we had always worked for. Her refusal to join me didn't infuriate me anywhere near as much as her statement that I didn't care what she wanted.

I grabbed the bottle of scotch off the counter behind her. I stood in front of her holding the bottle like a club. I don't know how long we stood there like that. I had no idea what she was thinking, but somewhere inside of me something clicked. I didn't know it at the time, but I can trace all the changes back to that moment.

I spun on my heels and walked out of the house. I drove for miles before I stopped, opened the bottle and drank half of it. When I got home, I sat in the garage and looked at the boys' bikes on the wall, at my tools beside them. Through the window I could see the swing set. Annie was swinging in and out of my vision. I went inside and called Steve and told him I didn't think the job was right for me right now.

We put all this aside, behind us, and we moved on. We slept together. We attended local band concerts together. At high school football and basketball games we could be found sitting side by side in the stands. Our children grew up while I worked six days a week and Carole kept the house and all our schedules running smoothly. In all, we were the picture of the perfect family. But somehow I don't remember looking at Carole from the day I stood before her with that bottle held like a club in my hand until sometime in the year before she died.

When the boys started college last year, Carole got a job.

She was one of the last women in the neighborhood to move into the job market. She started part-time at the Chamber of Commerce, but a little wasn't enough and soon she was there every day. The director of the chamber was an old school mate, Ken Jackson.

The day she took that job was the day I started looking at her again. What I saw was a face as smooth and self-contained as it was the day I watched her homemade petals droop around her hips. What I felt was the slow dawning of a feeling that could only be labeled shock. For as she told me of her days at work, her face growing ever more animated as she shed what she called her "hausfrau blues," the memory of desire stirred in me. I'm not talking about lust. I mean that desire to possess her.

I have photographs of her near a river, wearing jeans that hugged her hips and a top that stopped several inches above her navel, her hair long and shaggy on her shoulders, and a freshness in her face like nothing I have seen before or since. Even Anne, who is almost the mirror image of this younger version on her mother, lacks this intensity of light shining from a source as mysterious as the beginning of time.

I made love to her on the shores of that river in the dark outside a ring of firelight. But before that I photographed her, and she let me, with her breasts bare and the water lapping at her smooth brown skin. The photographer I was loved every nuance of shadow and light on her face. I took these pictures in hopes that I could possess her at the moment her image was imprinted on the film and again in the future when the photos became but a part of our shared history.

It sounds crazy, but I had forgotten all this. That day in the kitchen when she stood before me with the control so clearly in her hands, I had to turn away from her. I took back the control by feeling nothing. For years we had lived with that uneasy sort of truce.

I don't know. Maybe it was something as base as the thought of another man looking at her. Or something as simple as being alone in the house together after years of sharing it with kids and the noise that goes with them. Whatever it was, we started over. For us that meant she returned to her place on a pedestal and I watched her in awe. A grown man can't live that way.

After Fox hung up that day, I sat staring out the window for more than an hour. Then I walked out to the secretary's desk, told her to take a break: I needed her typewriter. I typed my letter of resignation, put it on the top of the secretary's desk with instructions on where to send it. Then I went back to my own desk, pulled my jacket off the back of my chair, took the photos of Carole, Annie, John and Josh off the desk and walked out of the office.

For four days I have been alone in this house with Carole's scrub bucket, mops, and brooms. I have become an expert on cleaning products I had previously known only by sight or smell. Now, stripped of pictures, furniture, rugs, closets emptied, shades drawn, the house rings with the hollow sound of my footsteps, smells only of a sterile cleanliness that masks any sign we were here. Only the last of Carole's plants, still hanging in the skylight, belie this image of our house as *tabula rasa.*

I have walked through this house, looked into each closet, on each shelf, into each drawer, and I am certain I have left nothing behind.

In the garage, my tools still hang on the pegboard wall. The back shelf still holds our camping gear, my hunting and fishing equipment, boxes of miscellaneous items too good to throw away but too bad to be of any use. On the east wall between the double door and the uncleaned window hang two fan rakes, one garden rake, a snow shovel, three spades, a posthole digger, and a hoe. Stacked in the corner and along the wall is the lumber left over from every project I have completed or planned for the past twenty-four years: one dog house, completed and lived in by three different dogs at three different times; a doll house, completed enough to suit me, but Carole remarked several times how little it resembled the plans; a skylight, started by me on a sunny June morning, completed on a threateningly gray late September afternoon by a home repair and general handyman whose ad I had seen in the barber shop. Paint cans, oilcans, gas cans and a lawn mower crouch along the wall.

This is my area. Everything here is where I put it. I am intruding on no one, invading nothing when I am here. I packed Carole's things methodically. She was always tidy and organized and it was easy to pack for her in the same way, to know who she wanted to have what.

Maggie, Carole's best friend, told me again and again she would help me pack, for Carole. Anne, who when young loved her dollhouse and didn't notice the missing walls, pleaded with me to let her do it during that long week she stayed with me after the funeral.

"Daddy," she had said. "Let me help. I can't bear to leave you like this." I wasn't sure then what "like this" meant. Both my sons offered, quietly, in a way I knew they were more afraid for themselves that I would say yes than they cared for me if that was what I needed. They offered because Carole had raised them well. I don't give her that – it's hers, there is no denying it.

It is a little like death, really, this moving from a house after all these years. It is only recent generations who have passed over to a stranger the rituals of preparing the body of a loved one for the grave. The Yellow Pages list more than half a dozen companies and individuals willing to clean up our daily dirt. I know I could have called one, any one, after packing the last box, moving the last table, putting the last chair into the van, to come and do this for me. But I harken to that earlier time when all was ours, from the very beginning to the very end.

At night I lie awake and wonder what Carole was doing that night. What was she thinking? How long did she stand there, before the car or pickup drove by and ended her life?

Unlike me, she frequently had trouble sleeping. On the night it happened I was in a deep sleep when I heard the shot. The bullet didn't fracture the entire window. It made only a small hole in the exact center, and the noise was limited to one sharp report and then a softer, rustling thud.

I would like to say that at the moment the bullet pierced Carole's brain I leaped out of bed and rushed to her side. But in truth, the sounds penetrated my own consciousness slowly and it was several minutes before the combination of the sounds and the fact of Carole's absence from the bed beside me created enough dissonance in me to get me up. I went to the bathroom before I went out to the kitchen and then to the family room. We so rarely use the living room that I didn't think to look for her there until after I had checked the garage for her car.

I was still considering how I might have reacted if I had not seen her car in its usual place when I found her. She lay crumpled on the floor, bathed in moonlight from the window. Her head haloed by her own blood. I remember I did the strangest things, like first saying, "Carole, come in here," as if I had found an unusual growth on one of her plants and I wanted her to see it. Then I leaned against the door jam and said, "Oh, Carole, Carole, Carole," in the same voice I used when she played the wrong card in our weekly game of pitch with the neighbors up the street. It took me several minutes before I could walk to her, take her wrist in my hand and confirm her death.

At last I have filled the last box. I stand for one last time in the living room, though I do not look down at the floor. Then I walk to the kitchen and look up at Carole's plants hanging in the skylight. I set the ladder up underneath them and climb until my head touches the top of the sun-filled dome. From this perch I look down through the leaves and I can see her watering them, standing on the counter leaning over to reach the furthermost ones. I can see her as clearly as I could see her blooming into the daffodil on the pedestal above me those long years ago.

I look up through the tinted glass of the skylight, see clouds scurrying along on the wind, feel I could touch them as easily as I had touched her.

Slowly I climb back down the ladder without taking down the plants. I look up through leaves and glass to see a jet trail bisecting the view. I decide to leave the plants, knowing it will be months before anyone comes back into this house.

SCAR

At the water's edge an old man stands skipping stones across the still, brown lake. We pass by him without speaking. Your hand in mine, passionless, we walk the length of the beach until we reach the bridge and the sand gives way to rocks to boulders to pilings. We stand and stare up at the bridge's underbelly and wait for a car to come, to shake the planks and scare the swallows and give us a reason to turn around and head back down the beach.

I want to say something to you now, while I have the chance. Something that has been knocking around in the back of my throat for days or years, but now while I have the chance the knocking has ceased. When I open my mouth to speak I am silent, my mouth agape like the baby birds in their muddy nests some fifteen feet above our heads.

You drop my hand suddenly and begin to climb across the rocks, up towards the road and I watch you, silently, of course. You have a goal and you are going toward it as surely as any goal you've ever had. I can't see anything up there that would make me want to climb either before or after you, but you do. You with your eyes turned toward horizons I've never even considered.

You slip your hand into a crevice and pull out a brown bottle. I don't know how you could have seen it to know it was there and I can't understand why you wanted it when you did see it. You hold the bottle up to the light, trying to peer through its opaque glass. Then you turn and smile at me, the smile of a conqueror.

I wait at the bottom, on the beach where the sand is still warm under my feet. I look back up the beach where the old man continues to try for a remembered rhythm of youth. I keep my back to you and wait. You left me, you can find your way back.

Eventually you do, with your treasure grasped in your hand.

"I thought it looked like it had something in it," you say. You hold it up for me to behold. I look, expecting liquid, but see paper folded neatly in accordion folds. "A message in a bottle!" you say. Your smile even bigger now, you look happier than you have in days. Nothing I've done to make you laugh or bring you pleasure has brought this little boy grin to your face, but now a piece of trash has uncurled your heart.

"Probably just the label," I say, turning to walk up the beach, to retrace our steps. But you don't follow and I know you won't before I've gone more than three yards. So I stop and look back at you. You are looking at the bottle, turning it over in your hands and trying to dislodge the paper with determined shakes.

I come back to you and stand beside you, both of us looking at this thing you have found.

"You'll have to break it," I say at last. And you do so, so suddenly I jump back startled by the ferocity of your throw. The glass shatters against a boulder near our feet, the shards making a blossom of brown crystals on the surface of the rock. The accordion-folded paper slides free. We both see at the same time that the paper is a note, handwritten scribbles on the entire surface. You reach to pick it up and I say, "Wait, first tell me what you think it says."

You laugh, suddenly more like yourself, and say, "How

the hell should I know." But you straighten back up, empty-handed, and turn to me. "What do you think it says?"

I look at your face, make note of the lines, the formation of which I had failed to watch. I note the scar, just above your left eye. The small question mark you got when the hammock we slept in gave way under our combined weight and the S-hook caught you there, marking you. I put my finger to that scar and look into your eyes, green with flecks of brown. You look like someone I used to know.

"I think it's some poor sucker's lament about unrequited love," I say.

"I think it's a message from someone on a deserted island," you say.

Same thing, I think.

You pick the paper up between thumb and forefinger, shake the slivers of glass free and unfold it.

I'm surprised to find myself holding my breath as I wait for you to read it, to tell me what it says, as if it were something that mattered.

"We're both wrong," you say at last. "It's loops." You hold it up for me to see, a sheet of connected loops, penmanship practice for someone. "It doesn't say anything at all." The disappointment in your voice so real even I can hear it.

I take the paper from your outstretched hand and study it closely. "But it could," I say, "It could." Suddenly the wind snatches it from my grasp and it skitters across the beach like a well-skipped stone. We stand side by side and watch the angle of its flight, like aging stone-skippers trying to recall the skill.

BACK SEAT

1

Riding in the back seat of our family station wagon my sister and I face backwards. Our father says this seat sits ass-backwards to the world and that description makes it all the more fun. We know the world looks different to us than it does to Mom and Dad in the front seat. Different because it is dark. Because it is receding. Because we have time to study it as well as anticipate it. Headlights of oncoming cars turn the shadow of our vehicle on the road behind us into a looming, crazy-looking and rapidly changing monster that pounces into nothing as the car passes. We make a game of it. We watch over our shoulders waiting for what's coming toward us then lean into the window, pressing our noses to the glass. We ooh. We aah. We scream and grab each other as the car passes. The monster pounces and we collapse to the floor in giggles. Our laughter, like grace it seems, rises up from beneath us, from inside and outside of this car. A bottomless supply.

2

Later, much later, I drive the car. The backward seat folded down to make room for baskets of laundry, groceries. My mother suddenly too sick, too tired, to keep doing what she has always done, jobs shift to me, the oldest girl still living at home. I don't mind. I get to drive the car. When my little sister asks to come along I say no. I'm picking up Jill or Marie or Debbie and there's no room for her, little girl to our sixteen.

They help me fold laundry at the Laundromat, Jill or Marie or Debbie. They take half my list at the grocery store and we race carts up and down aisles, not caring who we cut off or piss off in our hurry. Carving out time for a spin or two down Main we turn it all into a game. My mother never checks mileage. We can cruise out to Rabbit Road, share a smoke by the river, and be home before the ice cream melts.

3

My little sister comes home stumbling after football games, after play practice, after school. She wears black eye liner and dark blue eye shadow, nylon shirts snug tight across breasts suddenly round and firm. I find myself fascinated by her nipples. They are always erect, even when she's sleeping. Like antennae, they send signals I recognize but cannot articulate.

She doesn't ask to go with me anymore when I load laundry in the car. By the time I notice she's already gone. Men and boys in pickups and Camaros meet her at the corner, out of sight of our father's house. I see her sometimes when Jill or Marie or Debbie and I cruise Main. She curls up so close to whoever drives whatever car she's in that their shadows would have only one head.

4

The car needs a new transmission. As has always been the case, there's no money in the bank to pay for it. My dad's joke that he's too busy working to make any money isn't funny anymore. When he tells me I helped drive that car into the ground I can help pay for it, all my pleading doesn't change a thing. My little sister sneaks out the back door. The creak of the screen door audible only to somebody who is listening. Jill and Marie and Debbie leave for college. I get a job cleaning houses for Social Services. Most days I walk to work. The houses I clean are not far from home and nobody I know cruises Main these days.

5

My little sister's living in a two-room at the motel on the north edge of town with some guy who works for the railroad. I go to see her once when I think he's working. She only opens the door wide enough for us to see each other. I can hear a man's deep phlegm-filled cough from the dark behind her. Cigarette smoke hangs like gossamer in the flickering light of the TV. It's a school day and she's wearing the purple, terry-cloth bathrobe Mom and Dad gave her for her birthday last year. Sweet 16.

"At least he's got a job," my dad says when I tell him I'd seen her.

My mom and dad at the kitchen table playing cribbage. My dad's hands shake so my mom has to move his pegs for him. She's gone completely gray now and you'd never believe Jill or Marie or Debbie once told me she thought my mother was beautiful.

6

Outside the hospital I sit down on the first bench I come to. The doctor says my little sister will be okay. They stopped the bleeding in time. He wanted to know why I didn't bring her in sooner. Didn't I understand anything about sin? Did he really say sin? I try to recall exactly what was said in that room so brightly lit I didn't recognize my own reflection in the darkened silver of the towel dispenser. When the nurse asked me questions I had to admit I didn't even know the last name of the man my sister was living with. "Doesn't matter," my little sister had said behind me. "He's been gone for weeks." I looked at her face, pale against the white sheets, then at the nurse with her clipboard, and then at the ceiling where a fluorescent light buzzed and snapped like something dangerous was about to happen. "There's blood all over the front seat of the car," I said to no one in particular.

"What made you come today?" she had asked on the way here. "How did you know I was dying?" She leaned against the passenger window, her face as white as ashes.

"You're not dying, you goof," I had said back. But I could see her blood-darkened blue jeans and I pushed the gas pedal down. The engine ticked in protest.

Sitting now on the bench outside the hospital I wonder if it matters that I never meant to hurt anyone. Did the doctor really ask me if I understood anything about sin? I think about what made me go back to see her today. About how I just got in the car and drove over there without thinking, responding maybe to something both inside and outside of us that held us together.

7

The car gives up the ghost before the rest of us do. We're a family of walkers now whether we like it or not. That's why I have time to see the two little girls. They've been parked on a park bench by somebody who knew they were old enough to stay put. I watch them take turns tossing a rock onto each other's shadow. The older girl keeps making the younger one retrieve the rocks. She does it without complaint. They are both giggling. Laughing that bottomless laugh that little girls have. "Ooh, I got you in the head," they scream, oblivious to anything but themselves and their game. "Eeee, you hit me in the stomach!" They double over, reacting as if their shadows were themselves.

I walk backwards and watch them until their mother comes back. When they walk away, lagging a few steps behind her retreating figure, I find myself wanting to run after them. I want to grab the older one's arm. It's as if for a moment all I have to do is look back over my shoulder and I can see what's coming.

SCHOOL SHOOTING, MAY 1970

Joanna Eggerton stood at the office window watching the retarded kids clustered around the bus-stop sign. One of the boys looked as if he were trying to do some sort of Jerry Lewis routine, contorting his body in a strange, almost dance. But even Joanna couldn't find comedy in his actions. He couldn't stop if he wanted to. The one girl in the group, thirteen years-old and chubby, stood staring hard at the sign post some two or three inches in front of her nose. The other two looked normal from a distance.

Joanna took a long slow drag off her cigarette and shook her head slowly.

"When I started college I thought I wanted to be a special ed teacher," she said to no one in particular. She sent a smoke ring out to a moth caught between screen and storm window. "Now I'd rather be dead than have a classroom full of them."

Behind her, Carole Lamarr kept typing.

"You know what I mean?" Joanna turned toward her.

"My guess is that the kids would rather be dead than have you for their teacher," Carole replied in the same tone she would have used to recite a grocery list. She glanced up at the clock on the wall above Joanna's left shoulder then reached around to shut off her typewriter. She pulled the cover out of the bottom drawer of her desk and slipped it over the typewriter before standing up.

"Love to stay and chat," she said, "but it's lunchtime."

Joanna stood with her arms folded under her breasts, scrutinizing Carole with the same careful squint she had aimed at the kids at the bus stop.

"You're pretty cheeky for a secretary," she said.

Carole pulled her coat off the hook and wrapped it around her shoulders like a cape.

"Well, guess what Joanna," she said on her way out the door. "You ain't buttering my bread."

Joanna glanced up at the clock on the wall and then pushed up her sleeve to check the time on each of her three watches. She pursed her lips together in a straight line and stubbed her cigarette out in the ashtray at the edge of Carole's desk. Then with the eraser end of a pencil she pulled from behind her ear she gently spread the papers stacked beside the typewriter and looked over the top of her glasses to read what she could. Nothing interesting there but at the sound of the bell she jumped a little and looked back over her shoulder. The hallway was suddenly filled with kids. Kids who should be walking quietly were running and bumping into each other like wild things. Joanna strode into the hallway and clapped her hands twice. Two reports like gun shots silenced the kids in her immediate vicinity. The pocket of silence followed her down the hallway as kids elbowed the information one to another.

She paused at the door to the eighth grade home room and looked back up the hallway. Her eyes were gray, the color of cold. She pulled the door shut behind her and went to her desk at the front of the room.

From the bottom drawer on the left-hand side Joanna pulled out a rectangle of cloth and placed it on her desk. She spread it smooth with both hands then placed a quart-size thermos in the top right corner and a brown paper lunch sack in the center. She poured coffee, pulled her sandwich from the bag and sat with her head bowed for a moment. Bystanders would assume she was saying grace and in a way they would be right. Her eyes were closed and she was murmuring, "No. No. No," to the fear blossoming within her.

At precisely 12:15, Joanna looked up to watch her eighth-graders file back in from lunch. Despite the school's uniform rule the students had found ways to dress like bums, or what was it they were calling themselves now? Hippies. That's it. Hippies. One boy had altered his requisite dark pants by sewing a tapered strip of bright orange fabric in the outer seam from his knee to the cuff. Another boy sported a Nehru jacket and a pin that said "Make Love, Not War." She only let him keep it on because she didn't think he really knew what it meant. They're only thirteen, she would remind herself sometimes, though they seemed so much older than she had been at the same age.

The last two students to trudge past her desk were Nancy Taylor and Nancy Allen. She always thought of them as the two-tall too-tall Nancys. They had both had a growth spurt over the summer and had come back to school looking as awkward as they must have felt. Joanna knew what it was like to be the tallest person in a room, had known it since she was their age, but they didn't know that. They thought they were the first to feel what they felt, live what they lived.

The last class before lunch had been Home-Ec and most of the girls were carrying wads of fabric that they stuffed into their desks as soon as they sat down. The two-tall too-tall Nancys though had fashioned their projects, whatever they were supposed to be, into headbands. They were wearing them around their heads not like headbands should be worn, but around their foreheads like some ridiculous imitation of a drugged-up rock star. They giggled all the way to their desks, brave enough to plop the headbands on before they came into the classroom, but not brave enough to carry it off with any aplomb. Joanna watched them make their hump-shouldered way to their desks and shook her head.

It struck her suddenly that she couldn't remember what it felt like to love her students, to love teaching. She knew there had been a time, but she remembered it as fact, not feeling. Looking at these two now, two girls built like twins of herself at their age, she thought about how much she could teach them, how much she could tell them about what it was like to be them, if only they would listen. She felt a wave of sadness come over her, a wave of regret. She wanted her youth back. No, not youth. Desire. Love. Eagerness and ambition. She wanted to feel the way she did when she walked into her first classroom. As soon as the feeling came she started class.

"I see we have a couple of 'groovy chicks' with us this afternoon," she said as she stood up. "My, these two look like 'real hippies.' Aren't we honored to have them with us." When she first started talking she didn't think about where it might lead. Teaching was a spontaneous art form, she believed. Take what you have and mold it, make these lumps of life into citizens and you've led a good life. She just wanted to find a way in to the subject of the hour. History, it usually put them to sleep especially so soon after lunch. They still need an afternoon nap, she thought, they're such babies still.

Just a segue, that's all it was. When Nancy Taylor took her headband off, embarrassed by the attention, and Nancy Allen left hers on, fortified by it, Joanna thought a little battle of wills might spice things up a little. Make sense of history—it's all a record of battles anyway – by applying the present. Let's see who is stronger, who can outlast whom. She wanted to love her students, but if they didn't want to be lovable it was their loss.

"So where did we leave off last time?" she asked the class. "The beginning of World War I. Who can give me a summary of what's happened so far?" She looked around the room once or twice before settling her gray glance, as if by accident, on Nancy Allen's bowed head.

"You there, in the headband, maybe you could get us started."

The young girl's head ducked a little lower as if she thought she could hide even now, then she looked up at Joanna. She shrugged, "I don't know."

"You don't know?" Joanna feigned surprise. Eighth graders rarely offered information in discussions. "I thought perhaps the headband would help you hold your thoughts together a little better, but apparently I was wrong."

She looked around the room and asked anyone to volunteer a summary. In the silence she was struck again by her lack of feeling for her students. When she first composed this lesson plan she wanted to impart an understanding of how much the world had been changed by that war. "Before WWI," her youthful self had written in her lecture notes between the dates of battles and treaties, "people believed in the power of good to overcome evil. The world believed in its own ability to transcend itself. That is what made this war different from all the ones that came after it," she had written. She glanced down at those notes now and felt how naïve she had been. How foolish to believe she could learn about war, or teach it, from a book. Now, at best, she aimed to get them to remember who fought on which side and when.

"No takers?" she said at last. "Well, if you can't talk, at least you can listen." She launched into her lecture, focusing on the who and the when, staying clear of the why. She strayed from her notes only to occasionally bring the attention back to Nancy Allen. After the first attack the girl sat staring straight ahead, neither slouched nor rigid in her seat. She acknowledged the headband only when it began to slip down over her eyebrows.

When the students bolted from their seats at the sound of the bell, Joanna closed her notebook and watched them go, not even caring that Nancy Allen still wore the headband. She had five minutes before study hall duty. Long enough for a cigarette, she thought.

Carole Lamarr didn't greet her when she came into the office. She had the newspaper spread out in front of her and a coffee mug clutched in both hands.

"Must be break time all over the world," Joanna said as she held a match to her cigarette.

Carole looked up at her as if she hadn't noticed her before. "Have you heard about this?" she asked, gesturing toward the paper. Joanna glanced at the photos of bodies strewn on the ground and soldiers running. She blew smoke through her nose.

"The war," she said, "has been going on for quite some time. Haven't you noticed?"

Carole shook her head slowly. "This isn't Vietnam," she said quietly. "This is Ohio. These are college kids."

Joanna stepped around the back of the desk and started to read over Carole's shoulder. The two read in silence, speechless it seemed, until finally Carole spoke.

"Your son is in the National Guard, isn't he?"

Joanna's head shot up as if she had been struck.

"My son," she said, "my only son is a soldier in the United States Marine Corps." That's all she could say before the familiar wave closed her throat. She stared at the picture of a young girl crying. It's almost laughable, she thought, I could lose my son to this, to people who don't know the difference between one branch of the armed forces and another, to kids who don't know the difference between independence and rebellion. She brought her shaking hand up to her mouth and inhaled the last of her cigarette. She sent a cloud of smoke into Carole's face and turned to walk out the door. Carole's feeble apology unanswered.

In reality, the day after the Kent State shootings was no longer than any other, nor that atrocity any worse than the ones that occurred before or after. And there were and will be so many, so much worse than anyone expected. But Joanna could not get the picture of those particular students out of her mind, and each of her three watches seemed to have stopped. The angry, frightened faces made sense to her, but the looks of shock did not. What were they shocked about, she wondered. What did they expect to happen? If she could change anything, anything at all, what would she change?

These questions gnawed at her through the silence of study hall, and then the noise of PE where she stood on the sidelines and let the students run wild. They were still with her back in homeroom where she mumbled through the end of the day announcements. As a rule she checked the final bell against her watches, but today when it rang she simply sat down at her desk.

It was the two-tall too-tall Nancys that brought her back to the classroom. They were giggling into each other's humped shoulders. Both of them now wearing headbands. Nancy Allen's seeming victory had convinced Nancy Taylor that she too could wear the badge of independence.

Joanna blinked at their receding backs and almost, almost, let them go.

"Come back here, you two," she demanded suddenly. Her voice echoed in the almost empty room. "Off with the headbands," she said, "and don't wear them to school again."

Of course it was Nancy Allen who spoke up first. She swallowed audibly before asking, "Why? What's wrong with this style?"

She stared at Joanna with what might have been fear but looked like insolence to Joanna.

For an answer Joanna pulled a pad of pink detention slips from her desk. The girls didn't notice her shaking hands and Joanna didn't know how to keep them from shaking.

"Why?" Joanna said as she wrote out the first detention slip and tore it from the pad. "Why?" she wrote another and tore it off. She kept picturing the students strewn across the campus, bodies of rebels dressed just like these girls standing beside her. "Why?" she said again and again, tearing slip after slip off the pad and letting them pile up like body counts at the girls' feet. "Because," she said, as surprised as they were by the answer, "because I love you."

SEAMS

I almost didn't see it at all. I had gloves on so when my fingers grasped the mud-covered ball I didn't recognize it as anything but a clump of matted leaves. Scooped up onto the rake with broken branches and last fall's leaves, it would have been stuffed into a trash bag and gone forever if the phone hadn't rang right then. I was trying to stuff trash into a bag that wouldn't stand up while the cat rubbed against my leg and the sun got closer to disappearing faster than the yard was getting cleaned up, while that phone rang and rang and rang. I dropped the whole mess and ran inside. Wrong number.

When I came back out, there it was. The ball had rolled free of the leaves and the cat was nosing it as if she expected it to suddenly roll back into hiding again. As I picked it up my thumb found the X slashed into the leather and I knew what I had found. I remember David nursing his pinpricked thumb and telling me in his soft voice, Will was now his brother. He showed me where a little of their blood was mingled and rubbed into the ball. They were going to play major league baseball together, he had told me.

Sitting back onto my heels, I cupped my right hand around the ball and rubbed my thumb across the slash. Closing my eyes, I could hear his voice, see his face, how it looked the day the ball was lost. Angry at me, at himself, at the ball for not being where it should be, he tried so hard not to cry, but his eyes were shiny and his lip trembled.

"Mom. I have to have that ball. I can't play without it."

I swear we searched every inch of this yard. I don't know how it could have stayed hidden from us.

"Mom. You know it's my lucky ball. Find it!" His voice got higher at the end despite his best efforts to keep it low.

"I'm trying to find it," I told him. "Where did you put it? Are you sure you didn't take it with you when Jacob picked you up?"

My questions infuriated him and he began talking as if he were trying to get something through to a very dense person. It's hard to love a kid when he's acting that way. That he looked at me with his father's eyes made it that much harder.

"Dad was riding his motorcycle and we were going to a movie. Why would I take a ball along? I told you I left it right here." He jabbed his finger in the direction of the picnic table. "I left it with my glove. See," he held up his glove as proof of how right he was. "The ball should be with it." A car honked out front and his defiance turned to panic. "They can't be here yet!" He took just one step toward me. For a moment I thought he was going to run into the shelter of my arms, back into a time when making everything all right was as easy as a kiss. But he stopped. "I just can't go. I just can't play."

I didn't go put my arms around him.

"You know you have to go, David," I said softly. The car honked again. "I'll keep looking for it. Surely it will turn up."

"Will you bring it to me if you find it?" he asked.

"David, your game is thirty miles away and I have to be to work at 3:00." I tried to make it sound as if the logical answer to his question was in that statement.

"Will you?" he asked again. The car honked. He picked up his glove, but stood waiting for an answer.

"I'm sorry. No. But we'll find it before the next game."

We didn't, of course. And how it got from the picnic table where David knew he put it to deep inside the lilac bushes, I'll never know. We went over this yard again and again. The longer we looked the more frantic David's efforts became. Watching him search–stomping around the yard, standing on tiptoe to look into trees, lifting up the birdbath–was such a pathetic sight I wanted to cry for him.

The ball was an official Kansas City Royals baseball, actually hit by George Brett in person in practice. David's best friend, Will, had one just like it. In a fluke of fate, Brett had popped both balls into the stands right into the waiting hands of the two boys as if they were meant for them. David was sincerely proud of the large, purple bruise on his right hip that he got falling over the stadium seat trying to catch the one meant for him.

David's father had taken the two boys to a game the summer before and the boys came back fired up on baseball like they had gotten religion. They showed me how to practice holding the ball so that it was always ready to be thrown with maximum control.

"You gotta grab seams, Mom. That's what the professional pitchers do."

They walked around, sat around, laid around, tossing those balls up and catching them for weeks. Getting the feel of grabbing seams. They even took the balls with them to Little League, not to use, just as talismans.

Perhaps over time the novelty would have worn off and the balls would have become what they were, battered souvenirs of a time that would become not so much a memory as an idea of youth. But I have found that time doesn't move in a predictable, steady line, the way the calendars I use and schedules I make lead me to believe. It starts and stops and weaves around us in circles I don't always know how to move through. And every circle is filled with its own brand of sadness, so that I am never prepared for what comes.

Will and David had gone fishing with Jacob the day Beth, Will's mother, came over to tell me. I was re-sewing the inseam of David's blue jeans when she called to see if it was all right for her to come over. I told her yes, even though I didn't feel like having company right then. I was bitching out about Jacob, a frequent, if not favorite pastime of mine.

The fishing trip he and the boys were on was one of those surprises he liked to spring. He had stopped over just before supper, pulling a brand new bass boat behind his recently purchased Jeep Cherokee, to see if David could go out to the lake with him. A phone call first would have taken too much time. The fact that I had supper in the oven was no problem; they would pick up burgers on the way out of town. Of course David could go with him. Why should I always play the villain?

"Promise me you boys will wear your life vests," I had said to David before they left. "Even if your dad doesn't." He and Will were so excited about the prospect of riding in the new boat I had to grasp David's shoulders to make him look at me when I spoke to him.

"You boys be careful." I said this firmly, hoping to impress the importance of self-reliance on his mind. "You take care of yourselves."

"Oh, Mom," David said with the tone of a worldly eleven year-old. Then he kissed my cheek and raced out the door to catch up with Will. I followed them out. When I saw them hook their seat belts without being told I felt a little better about letting them go.

I walked over to where Jacob was checking the straps on the boat.

"You must have come into some money," I said. "I hope that means I can be expecting a little of the back child support."

"Don't start with me, Kate," he said.

"Where were you with that advice twelve years ago?"

He gave the safety strap one last tug and walked away without responding.

That scene started me on my rendition of the single parent

blues. When I started sewing after supper I kept the rhythm going by jamming the needle into the denim with each stressed syllable of each complaint. I was sew-ing a pair of Da-vid's blue jeans for the third time be-cause I could-n't af-ford to buy him a-nother pair.

When I jammed the needle into my finger so far only the hardness of the bone kept it from coming out the other side I forced myself to slow down, on the sewing, at least.

My mother used to say sewing relaxed her. "When things get too rough," she would say, "I just pick something out of my sewing basket and get to work. 'Now here's something I can fix' I say to myself."

As for me, sewing only reminds me of all the things I can't fix.

My parents died in a car crash two years after my marriage failed. By inheriting their house I had shrugged the worry of how to pay rent without any financial support from David's father. However, I shouldered a responsibility I had no idea was waiting for me: standing on the front line of mortality, a twenty-nine year old orphan.

And now Jacob, whose parents send post cards from Minnesota in the summer and presents from Phoenix at Christmas, was out with his latest girl friend and my son. The pettiness of resenting my ex-husband for having healthy, living parents was not lost on me, but once I got that needle stuck in the self pity groove I was going round and round with it whether I liked it or not. They say time is the great healer, but I think that's true only if we're allowed to forget. If I could get Jacob out of my life, I could forget and be healed. But we have a son.

When Jacob shows up here with one of his girl friends the knot I get in the pit of my stomach doesn't come from jealousy or resentment. I no longer begrudge him his sex life. I'm just afraid of the things he teaches David. He appears in David's life like rushes of adrenaline. For David, time with his father is frenetic in its pacing, like this last minute fishing trip. He comes home from each visit exhausted, drained of energy, but pumped up with promises.

"I'll see you this weekend," I have heard Jacob say when he dropped David off. "Have your camping gear ready." But the weekend will come and go with no sign of Jacob. David will be afraid to leave the yard or even take a shower for fear he will miss his dad's call.

Jacob's visits are determined by his own sporadic need for contact with a little boy who worships him. He shows David only the excitement of a life lived on your own terms. Sure that's a great theory. But what about the people who get hurt? Like the son who watches an empty street, or sits beside a silent phone. Every hurt I saw David endure burned an indelible pain into my heart. I guess that's a big part of this parenting job: feel every slight your child suffers, then magnify it to ulcerous proportions.

Beth startled me out of my litany of complaints when she knocked on my door. What she told me that day made me question whether having a child was worth all the pain, and it made me need David more than my next breath. I was so afraid of her words I could hardly bear to touch her when she began to cry. I was irrationally and selfishly afraid that somehow the tragedy in her life would rub off on me.

Will didn't know yet. He knew something was wrong. He was tired too often not to know, but Beth had delayed telling him how bad it was. The doctors said they had to start treatment right away and now she couldn't put it off any longer. I didn't know how to help her tell her son, and I hoped I would never have to learn. Somehow, I think she understood that. When we cried in others' arms that day our tears washed out of the familiar fear of the fragileness of our sons' lives. We cried from the knowledge born in us when we became mothers, knowledge that is pain.

Will was bedridden by the time David lost the ball. David didn't tell him it was lost. When Will made David promise to think of him when he hit that ball in the major leagues David told him he would, he promised.

He stopped looking for the ball after Will's funeral. He

seemed to shut the door on that part of his life. At first I thought it was just too painful for him to think about Will. I let him work out his grief in his own way, but as time went on I began to suspect that he wasn't hiding his grief. He wasn't feeling it at all. A part of me wanted to see him cry, just once. Maybe just so I would know he knew how to love. But I didn't even see him look sad. He took up new friends, played more baseball, perfected his Nintendo skills and looked more like his father every day.

The phone calls to girls were what really got me. If it were just one or even two girls it wouldn't have hit me so. But he seemed intent on building up a harem. All my fears about what Jacob's lifestyle had taught David came bubbling to the surface. At the rate he was going I was sure he was someday going to end up in a marriage that ended up like his father's. The girls in David's life didn't seem any different from the girls in Jacob's. The girls who stand like dominoes stretching in a line from before the end of our marriage to the present.

Jacob's girls. I think the first one's name was Cheryl. What I mean is, I know her name was Cheryl, I think she was the first one. I met her at the Memorial Day picnic the year David turned four. After I had some time to get used to it, I sort of appreciated the irony of having my marriage end on Memorial Day. Its not as obvious as having a baby on Labor Day, but it has its own sort of humor.

Cheryl was wearing a yellow silk tank top and a pair of faded Levi's with the knees ripped out. This was before torn clothing was the rage, so I thought she was either very brave, or very poor. Which ever it was, she was also very beautiful. One belt loop on those Levi's was torn loose at the top and hung uselessly below her rope belt. I remember the torn belt loop because it is what made everything unravel.

When I first saw them together, they were standing beside the pickup where the sound system was set up. They had their backs to everyone, looking at tapes, I guess. They started laughing about something and Jake reached out, grabbed that belt loop and pulled her toward him. Their hips touched only for a moment, but the action was as intimate as a kiss. He hadn't even looked for the loop when he reached out. It seemed to me there was a memory in his hand that led him to that loop, that spot on her body.

Later, when Jake helped me carry boxes from the car I asked him who she was.

"The blonde?" He said it as if he were debating whether to act ignorant or innocent. "Oh her. That's Dan's little sister."

"I didn't know he had one."

"Yeah. She goes to school here."

"Does she live with Dan?"

"Nope." He was getting very involved with unloading the car, but I kept my pace up with his, working beside him, trying not to sound panicky.

"How is it you know her?"

"She plays with us once in a while when the guys get together."

"Oh, she plays, does she?" I said, remembering how her breasts moved beneath her yellow silk top.

"Yeah, wait'll you hear her play the mandolin."

"Oh, you mean she plays an instrument," I said. I think that was the moment Jake knew that I knew, but he let it go. For the rest of the day he found a lot to do that kept him away from me. I went from numb to angry to scared to numb again in those next few hours. I didn't know how to act or what to say. It wasn't a surprise to me, really, but still it shocked the hell out of me. I was afraid I would do something that would make me look like a bad actress in a B movie so I ended up not doing anything at all. I watched David intently so I wouldn't have to see anything else. I watched him watch ants. I watched him swing, his plump legs pumping furiously to get the swing to move in a two-foot arc. I kept my eyes glued to his every action, as if seeing his innocence could restore my own.

I think if he hadn't taken a nap I would never have spoken to Cheryl, but with my son out of my line of vision I didn't have anywhere else to look but at that belt loop.

We were cleaning off the serving table after supper when we ended up beside each other. I didn't say, "So you're sleeping with my husband?" A restraint I viewed as admirable. Instead I said, "So, you're a mandolin player?"

"Yeah, I guess," she laughed. She didn't seem at all nervous in my presence—which struck me as being unbelievably cheeky at the time. "I'm not very good, but the guys put up with me."

"Do you play with 'the guys' much?" I tried to keep the quotation marks out of my voice.

"During the past school year I've been jamming with them once or twice a week. Tonight's the first time I'll play with them in public, though," she said. "Do you play?"

"No, not really." I had a perverse need to work Jake's name into the conversation. "Jake's tried to teach me, but apparently I'm hopeless."

"Oh, do you know Jake?" She showed genuine surprise.

"Sort of," I answered. "I'm his wife."

Two red spots appeared just below her cheekbones, as if someone had pressed his thumbprints onto her face. The appearance of the dots made me change my mind about wanting to hit her. Seeing them made me realize that she was not the enemy.

"Jake's married?" Her voice was a little too bright. She didn't look at me and she didn't stop setting the food into the cooler. "He never mentioned that." Until that moment I still had hope, but Cheryl's sudden paleness told me everything I didn't want to know. I turned around, walked to the car and crawled in beside my sleeping child. I pulled him into my arms, measuring my breathing to match his. As long as I held him in my arms, I felt I could keep from going under.

I wanted so badly for our marriage to work I tried to believe Jacob's affair was some kind of accident. I thought if I tried hard enough I could bridge the gap between us and we would be the happy family I thought we were. But something ugly and destructive had been set into motion when I wasn't looking and by the time I turned to face it I was powerless to stop it.

When I picked up the ball and held it in my hands, I felt as if I had found something precious. I pulled away wet, matted leaves and rubbed the ball on my leg to clean off the mud. I rolled it in my hand and grabbed a seam. And I thought about David. I thought how from the moment he was born I had recognized everything about him, even when I didn't understand him. I was so young when I first held him, I guess we grew up together.

But in the past year something had changed, something more than just growing up. He was changing every day; already he was as tall as I. Sometimes when he stood beside me I got the feeling he was about to shoot up, out of my reach. I had begun to fear that if I didn't reach him soon, he would be lost to me. He would become a part of a strange and alien world where people do not touch or need each other and I would have no place.

But I had found this ball. I thought, hoped, maybe I had found a key. Maybe this was the thing I needed to unlock the part of David that I knew, that was a part of me.

I found him in the kitchen when I went into the house. He stood in front of the refrigerator, his arm hooked over the open door, pondering the contents. I swallowed the urge to tell him to get what he wanted and close the door.

"You just get home?" I asked.

"'Bout five minutes ago," he said into the cool interior. "Don't we have anything to eat in this house?"

"Well, let's see." I stepped up behind him and peered over his shoulder into the refrigerator. "There's chicken. There's lunchmeat. There's lettuce. There's cheese. There's soup. There are eggs. There's casserole. There are apples. There are oranges. Nope. Poor us. Not a single thing to eat in this house."

He scowled over his shoulder at me and grabbed an apple before slamming the refrigerator door.

"Look at this," I said, extending the ball toward him. He was looking through a cupboard and only glanced at what I held in my hand. "I found it in the lilacs." I continued to hold the ball out to him until he finally turned toward me and took it from my grasp.

"Huh," he said, looking at the ball. He's going to toss it up in the air and grab seams, I thought. He rolled the ball onto the table and turned back to the cupboard. I sat down and tried not to feel disappointed. I told myself I wasn't looking for a big emotional scene. I just wanted to open a door. He grabbed a bag of potato chips off the counter and started to walk out of the room.

"Don't you want to take this?" I said, rolling the ball toward him.

"I guess so." He picked up the ball and walked into his room. Before I had a chance to decide what I felt or what I was going to do the phone rang. Of course David picked it up before the second ring. I heard him tell someone, sure, he'd be right over. I didn't look up at him when he came back into the kitchen.

"That was Rick," he said. "He got a new Nintendo game he wants me to try. Is it all right if I go over there?"

I nodded my head and he walked out the door. His footsteps receded across the porch and then I heard the crunch of both feet landing on the gravel. I sat in the empty kitchen and tried to collect my thoughts, but nothing clear would come to me.

Finally I stood up. I didn't think, I just felt angry when I went into his room, I had to be to go in there. I had raised him on the right to privacy and stomping into his room now when I knew he wouldn't catch me was a breach of faith I never thought I would commit. But something in me wouldn't let this go. I knew he had probably just tossed the ball onto the dresser or under the bed and I would be damned if I would let it disappear again. I looked on the dresser first, then on the bed, even tossed pillows around a little bit trying to find it. I looked on the floor in the closet and on the shelves. When I dropped down on my hands and knees to look under the bed I was fuming. He was just like his father, I thought. Relationships don't mean shit to him. Love who you're with and to hell with those out of sight. He had had something special with Will, a friendship that could have lasted a lifetime, that did last a lifetime for Will and David didn't even know enough to cherish it.

Under the bed I found balled up socks and balls of dust, but no baseball. I came up fast, determined to find that ball and keep it some place special, and caught my shoulder on the partially opened bedstand drawer. I slammed it shut to punish it for hurting me and something rolled back, hit the back of the drawer and then rolled forward and back again. When I pulled the drawer open, the ball rolled forward and came to rest on a photograph. I picked up the ball and the photo and sat down on the edge of the bed.

The photo was bent and smudged, as if it had been handled and looked at many, many times. They must have been eleven when the picture was taken. It was before Will started chemotherapy because his hair is thick and wavy and hangs in his eyes. They are sitting on the picnic table under the oak tree. The leaves have just started to change. David is leaning behind Will, holding two fingers up behind his head. They are both laughing and their faces are so full of life and youth it is incomprehensible that anything dark could ever touch them. Impossible to believe that when the moment was frozen on film, Will's body was killing him. Will is holding a bat, David, a glove. On the table between them are two baseballs.

A wave of guilt rushed up from my stomach and turned my face red. Not just because I was here, in David's room, uninvited. But because I'm a fool.

I don't know how much time passed before I put the ball and photo back into the drawer and stand up. For a moment I stay at the door, thinking about my son, about the soon-to-be-a-man who lives in this room, and I know he is not me. And he is not Jacob. I closed the door, softly, yet the click echoes throughout the stillness of the house.

WHAT COMES OF THIS?

We were spinning, my daughter and I. Spinning in circles with our arms out wide, our heads back and mouths open like baby birds in a nest. She wore red pants, a pink and purple striped shirt, green cowboy boots and a yellow straw hat pulled down hard over her blonde ponytails. Her colors stayed in the corner of my eyes, that sacred space, and she became a kaleidoscope. We spun ourselves in circles like living tops until our knees gave out and we fell, laughing into grass and wildflower. Then the earth took up our dance, as it does when you've grown too dizzy to hold yourself still. Stretched out amidst bluestem and buffalo grass, cone-flowers and tickclover, we felt the spin of this planet through space. Out of my sight on the other side of plants tall and short my little girl called out laughing, I'm still spinning round and round.

I can remember the exact tickle of foxtail against my right ear, the exact slant of the spin of that fall and the high sound of my daughter laughing as she discovered the pull of this blue ball spinning here on the edge of this galaxy. I can remember how joy of the moment felt like air and light. There was space unfathomable in my chest, my particular chest, and I let the sound of her laughter into that space. Smiling up at the sky I held onto it, all of it, a rare moment of not thinking about what comes next or what came before.

It was in the silence between breaths, in the catch between inhaling and exhaling, that I turned toward the sound of my daughter laughing, the grass tickling my right ear and cheek. Turning my head toward the sun of her I saw, beside me in the grass and wildflower, a hand. A human hand with fingers white, long and limp lying beside my spinning face. I caught my scream in my throat to keep from frightening my little girl. My first thought beyond horror was of her. I sat up to see her still laughing into the cosmos while beside me the long white fingers of someone else's daughter stretched out into the roots of the meadow grass.

Only after I knew my daughter was safe, when I knew it was not her hand stretching toward my face, could I look again through the rustle of leaves and blades of grass to see what I saw. My breath stopped again when I saw the hand stopped at being just a hand, did not become a body, did not become a person. I felt a deep coldness in my fingers and face. I closed my eyes and waited for equilibrium.

When I was able to look again, to look closer, I saw what I should have seen from the first. A root, a tuber, the secret, ancestral part of a plant clutched the earth, even as my daughter and I had after falling. Not a hand at all. I laughed out loud, almost crying. I stood up, no longer dizzy, and reached out my arms, making impossibly long shadows in the late afternoon light, and caught up my little girl, my baby, my future. I held her to my chest, my beating heart, and I hugged her, spinning. We twirled with the sun and the wind and when we fell, the planet, this particular planet at this particular moment in space and time kept spinning beneath us. I kissed my daughter's eyelids, her nose, the blade of her particular jaw, young and barely formed, and in the catch between letting air in and back out again, I knew: we too shall become dust.

CHARLEY AND EVELYN'S PARTY

The pink roses in the pattern of her dress are as big as a man's fist. The purse she carries is a small oval box banded in gold with a large gold clasp that snaps discretely when it closes. It looks like a child's purse and makes her look even more vulnerable than the way she smiles. She came with the Flaherty's, Pat and Marie, and they keep her a part of things, making sure she is introduced to everyone at least once. Marie calls her Ruth, but Pat forgets several times and calls her simply "Joe's widow."

You could tell just by looking at her that she had rushed to get ready, had held that purse in her hands and watched the empty driveway for twenty minutes before the Flahertys had arrived. You know too that the empty driveway made her doubt her decision to go to this party. Maybe she noticed the seashell button on her dress looked loose, the one between her breasts. Last time she wore it Joe had pulled it, pretending he could hear the sea. Maybe she thought to fix it but the Flaherty's came and time to go took all thoughts but hurry from her head.

The party: a surprise for Charley and Evelyn's fortieth wedding anniversary. But Charley is in the hospital with kidney stones. He fell ill too late to cancel the party. Fifty-some people invited to a potluck dinner. The family, together for the first time since Christmas two years ago, held an emergency conference and decided to substitute a video camera for their father. The camera is traded from shoulder to shoulder of Charley's sons and daughters for most of the night. They introduce the camera as Charley and guests talk to it. Some say how bad they feel that he couldn't be here, hope he's feeling better. Others treat the camera as if it were Charley, making jokes about how much better he looks, how much weight he has lost, maybe even grown some hair back.

Charley and Evelyn's son, Thomas, from San Francisco, is here with his gay lover. Simon is the only black man at this party but he doesn't seem to notice. When it is Thomas' turn to carry the camera he starts at the buffet table and pans the selection of food. I made your favorite, Dad, he says to the camera. Simon tilts a crockpot filled with barbecue ribs toward the camera. That's my favorite, too, Simon says. My mom used to make them like that. Thomas sticks his hand out in front of the camera and points his thumb down. I'll turn you both into vegetarians before I'm through with you. Simon laughs and says, no way. I'm with you Charley, give me steak or give me death.

Charley and Evelyn's oldest daughter, Linda, appears beside her brother's lover and takes his elbow lightly. Dad's not even here and you two are ganging up on my poor baby brother, she says to Simon. She steers them away from the food table. Be sure to get a picture of my handiwork, she says, and points toward the back of the patio where a figure is propped up beside the light post.

A cardboard figure wearing a golf shirt and Bermuda shorts sits in a folding chair, a can of beer duct-taped to its cardboard hand. The face, drawn with magic marker, bears a striking resemblance to Charley. Evelyn poses beside the caricature of her husband while cameras flash. When Thomas arrives with the video Evelyn turns toward him and speaks to the camera, I don't know Charley, this guy's a better listener.

You better hurry back before I decide to keep this new version. You have to look closely to see there are tears in her eyes. It is late by now so it's no surprise when someone, one of Charley's golfing buddies, calls out a joke about the new version being better in the sack too. Evelyn laughs in mock horror and puts her hand over the lens of the video camera. I've got grandkids who'll be watching this, she says. You be good.

Pat Flaherty steps up then and takes the camera from Thomas. Let's get those grandkids in here, he says. Let's get Charley and Evelyn's family together for a group shot. He starts calling for kids and grandkids and waves them over as if he were directing this show. The camera, still on, dangles at his side, filming grass and feet. When the video is watched later you will be able to catch a glimpse Joe's widow. She has slipped off her shoes and is rubbing a corn on her right foot.

From out of nowhere it seems kids come running. Pat pulls the camera up just in time to catch the oldest grandchild, a lanky boy of ten, swing down from a tree limb and land beside his grandmother. Evelyn screams first then hugs him. She pulls a chair up beside the cardboard figure of her husband and reaches up for the baby, her newest pride. Linda sits at her feet and pats the ground for her husband to join her. Thomas steps in behind his mother, pulling Simon with him. He doesn't want to come, but to refuse would make a bigger scene. James, the oldest son, stands back for a moment too long, watching Simon. Pat handles the camera loosely. He never quite gets everyone into one shot, but at that moment, no one knows that.

The sky is dark now. But in the city like this you can only make out a few of the brightest constellations. Cassiopeia and the Big Dipper hang just above the pine trees in the back yard. A shooting star marks its short-lived trail just under the North Star. Ruth twists the seashell button on her dress and it comes off in her hand.

CROSSINGS

Madeline watches as Dara picks her way gingerly down the path. Shoeless, Dara places each foot with care until she reaches the wooden dock. She knots her towel around the railing, pauses for a moment, feels her mother's eyes on her back, then dives into the icy waters of Lake Atwanbe. The first contact shocks and she feels herself come fully awake. She pushes herself forward beneath the water's surface with one strong thrust and lets the momentum carry her as the water around her grows calm again. The moonlight shines too thinly to penetrate the surface of the water. She stays there in complete darkness as long as her breath will hold because she loves the feel of almost not reaching the surface in time, loves the moment when the desire to breathe becomes so strong it becomes pain and the surface still so far away, too far, her mouth opening in preparation for the final surrender, and then the break into air, the gasp for life.

At the window where she stands watching, Madeline breathes again also. She moves her hand feebly to brush off the specter of her daughter's not returning and a white hand waves back from the water.

There come times when they let loose of one another, breathe separately, but for now they see directly into one another's eyes, though Madeline only a shadow at the window, Dara one small dot in the placid waters twenty feet from shore.

In the lake, Dara swims closer to the shore, peels her swimming suit down and throws it onto the dock with a wet splat. Freed, her one, ponderous breast floats weightlessly upward. She feels a slight sting between her legs where the briny water touches her. Suspended there she lets herself feel the dark water on her skin. She recalls the feeling of being entered from behind by a lover whose face she cannot see but who fills her and calls her name. The memory of it forces her down again beneath the surface. Hand out, she tries to touch the bottom, but she is past the shelf and her breath won't hold. At the last moment she breaks upward again.

They both gasp for air.

In the morning they will not speak of midnight swims. They will comment on the hint of fall in the morning air, on how alive the fog appears as it ascends into nothingness, on what to buy at the market for tonight's dinner. They will cook, wash dishes, wash and iron clothes, sweep floors, water plants. The multitude of chores that once got in the way of living will be for now the measure of their days. They will be only mother and daughter.

"You frighten me," Madeline says, looking down into the face shining white against the black water. She stands on the dock, her bare toes curl around the wooden edge, an afghan hugs her shoulders like a cape.

"Security is an illusion, Mother. You told me that yourself."

"Yes, well, I got that from Helen Keller and who's to say you can trust her?"

The younger woman laughs, surprised by the other's cryptic tone.

"Join me," she says. "It's not as cold as you make it seem, huddled up there like the French Lieutenant's Woman."

Madeline gazes out across the water and inhales deeply.

"They say there was another sighting last week down in Wilson's Bay," she says in reply. "That's the closest it's been in years."

"Well hurry, jump in, maybe it's our turn. I've been feeling terribly lonely of late."

This time Madeline's laugh rings out across the water like a young girl's. She had almost forgotten this family exchange. The local myth of a sea creature in this Canadian lake had once frightened her children into night terrors and swimming phobias. To calm them she made up her own stories about this mysterious creature. In the telling the creature lost its power to frighten and became instead whatever they needed it to be: a scapegoat, a confidant, a potential, ideal suitor. Through the stories she told, the children, and Madeline too, learned to share their world with things they didn't understand. But the stories had always been told on the safety of the shore. Even when they laughed they did not let go completely of the fear. It waited somewhere inside each of them, making them keep their distance from this thing they had never seen, knew only through stories.

"You're wicked," Madeline says, smiling. She looks out over the dark water and then around her once before she drops her afghan, revealing her nakedness. A spider's web of stretch marks crosses her belly, breasts, and thighs. A deep red scar on her right leg reminds her daily of a long-ago car accident, making her careful in all things. The crease along her lower abdomen marks her children's first home. Still she moves with the lightness of a young woman as she dives into the water. Together the women swim beneath the surface, daring one another to stay just a little longer, to stay in the embryonic underworld as long as their lungs can hold. They burst through the surface at exactly the same time, laughing and gasping.

"Let's make a train," Dara says when she catches her

breath. She pulls a float off its hook at dock's end. "Remember how we used to do this, the whole family? I thought we could float for hours and go for miles doing this. This time, though, I want to be the engine."

The two line up, Madeline's back to Dara's front. Dara leans back onto the float and brings her legs up under her mother's arms. Madeline rests her head on Dara's belly and lets her feet rise to the surface. Nestled together they float in the darkness.

"I remember looking out at all of you in this line, spreading out from between my legs, and I was always amazed at the sight. I could never quite believe you all came from me, had once been in me. And yet there we were, our arms and legs entwined so that I couldn't tell where one of us stopped and the other started." The lap of water on their skin and on the shore is hypnotic in the darkness.

"Do you ever know?" Dara asks. Her face turned upward toward the distant moon.

When Dara was small, her needs were few and basic. Madeline filled them as she was able. Through the simple steps of daily living they found some laws of nature did not hold. Once, in a surreal moment, they gazed into one another's eyes. Infant mouth locked onto mother's breast, they saw one another fully. Madeline saw the graceful arc of the underside of her own breast, her own face gazing back at her. Dara beheld herself through the lens of a mother's love. Not to be believed, not to be talked about, not to be forgotten. When the moment of crossing came again Dara was less than three. She sat at the kitchen table drinking milk from a cereal bowl while Madeline watched and suddenly saw the bowl up close to her own eyes, saw the pale reflection of the child's face looking back at her from the inner whiteness of the bowl. When the milk was gone, the little girl, suddenly wise, set the down the bowl, smiled at her mother and went out to play.

In the cool, dark water Dara turns from the moon and looks down across her own body to where her mother's head rests. In the water and the pale moonlight, with her mother so close to her, she can almost ignore the scars on her chest, the missing breast. "Do you ever really know?" she asks again.

"I suppose," Madeline replies, "the one who lives on after the other dies will know."

And so it is that they begin to learn to speak of death. They will stumble, have difficulty getting started, wonder what it is they should say to one another, what it is that they know, feel, want. These are the facts: the moments they have known are past, the time they have together fleeting, the future an unknown. Yet they feel something beyond facts, beyond words. They have come here, to this place, this time, to feel their way into an unknown, holding the flame of themselves against the darkness.

〜∞〜

"Tell me a story," Dara says. She stands behind her mother, her strong fingers twisting strips of Madeline's gray hair into a single thick braid that reaches almost to her waist. Madeline straddles a chair. Both face the open water where the morning mist writhes as it rises, moves like spirits beneath their watchfulness.

The story Madeline remembers is this: She is a child of nine, alone under an azure winter sky. The world around her is starkly colored: white snow, black trees, blue sky. The only sounds, her own breathing, her feet crunching on the snow. With the abandon known to children she spreads her arms wide, looks upward toward the heavens and falls backward, the jolt of body meeting earth softened by the thick blanket of snow. She swims her arms and legs in the crystalline whiteness, then carefully stands and steps away from her creation.

Behind her the snow angel rises also. Silently without a glance at her creator the angel gets up and walks away, its shoulders hunched against the cold. The little girl of nine alone under an azure winter sky watches the figure disappear in the woods north of the house. She doesn't call it back, ask it where it is going, say, 'wait, what about me?' Instead, she watches it walk away in silence.

When she became a mother she believed she already knew how to let go of her children, how to let them choose their own way, the angel had taught her that much, but now, faced with the profound prospect of loss, she knows there is more to learn. It is the more she cannot find the words for. So impossible to talk about what she doesn't know.

Dara twists a red elastic ribbon around the end of the braid, smoothes her hands over Madeline's hair, then picks up her coffee cup and holds it in both hands. Madelines's eyes are still closed.

"Tell me a story, Mother. The one you don't think you can."

"No, not yet," she answers slowly. "Do you remember our first summer here? You were five and as wild as all your brothers put together. Your father worried himself sick watching the four of you make your way around the water's edge. I stayed as close as I could without teaching you fear, but somehow I knew even then you were all safe as children, that we would grow old together. It was that sea monster that taught you all to respect the unknown."

While they talk each of them busy their hands with the tasks of morning. Madeline sweeps the kitchen floor. Dara washes dishes.

"Did you know about the monster before you bought the property?" Dara interrupts.

"Oh, we had heard rumors, but in those years when they were opening the lake for development no one who had anything to gain wanted to talk about that old myth. The old-timers who didn't have anything to gain didn't believe in it so what we heard was pretty spotty. I've never been sure that the so-called sightings were anything but part of the battle between the old-time landowners and the developers. The people who wanted everything to stay exactly as it had been since the beginning of time and the people who wanted change and money with it."

"I was absolutely terrified of that monster when I was little," Dara says. She puts the last of the dishes into the cupboard and walks to the window to look out at the lake.

"I know," Madeline laughs. "I have to admit that a part of me didn't want to discourage your fear. I didn't have to worry so about you children when you were worried yourself."

"That's such a Mom Trick."

"I know. Sometimes I feel that's what motherhood was, a series of tricks that led to all of you growing up." She puts the broom away in the hall closet and says over her shoulder, "I didn't think of them as tricks, you know, I just did what I needed to do. What I could do." Then, without spoken agreement, the two of them walk toward the bedrooms and begin making beds, one on each side smoothing the sheets and blankets.

"We chose this cabin because your father liked the idea of going to another country every summer," she continues. "Even though we're only 200 miles from home and the scenery is the same, we've come to another country."

She makes her voice low and gruff. "'It demands that you pay attention to the subtleties of difference,' your father said when we first saw it. 'Big changes are easy to see but life is full of the little changes that can slip by without your noticing if you're not careful.'"

"He's so much more romantic and philosophical in your stories than he is in real life, you know," Dara says, plumping a pillow and tossing it onto the bed between them. "I really can't imagine the busy businessman I know saying anything about 'the subtleties of difference.'"

"Well, both sides of him are true. I only tell you what I see." Madeline is stung by her words, though she's not sure why. A catch forms in her throat but she goes on as before.

"Anyway, we bought this place, monster or no. We have lived our life together carefully, making note of the big and little changes. Some things got by us, of course." She smiles wryly at some unnamed memory.

"Would you have wanted to know everything?" Dara asks.

Before she can stop herself her eyes flick down to her daughter's chest. Alone here with just the two of them, Dara has not disguised her loss and the right side of her T-shirt lies flat against her skin.

"Not everything," Madeline answers, "but some things I wish I had known earlier."

Dara watches her mother's face in silence for a moment. How did they find themselves here so suddenly?

"It's not your fault, you know."

Madeline gazes back into this face she loves and knows so well and wants to believe her.

"But I would take the blame if it would keep it, all, away from you," she says.

"There are no bargains to be made, Mother. No one to make them with anymore, you taught me that yourself," Dara answers.

It is then that the catch in Madeline's throat grows and threatens to choke her. She feels the terror of her mother-power, her decisions, her stories.

But that's just it, she wants to say. What if I've been wrong? What if everything I taught you is wrong? What have I left you with?

When the decision was made to meet one another here, they did not say why they needed to come to this cabin, why they needed time alone together. Though they had said Cancer, had said Death, neither had found the words to say Life. Though they are both still searching for whatever it is that will show them the way to take that step, Madeline knows that her own doubt is not the road to take.

Dara breaks the silence stretching between them.

"Remember the snow angel story, Mother? The one that walked away?"

"Your memory is crowded with my stories. I'm afraid." Madeline answers. She walks back to the kitchen. Dara follows.

"Oh don't be afraid," Dara laughs softly. "I'm very selective. If I'd kept them all, I'd never have had any fun in college."

"Now there are some of those things I'm better off not knowing." She laughs too, feeling the reprieve of another, safer, topic.

"Tell it to me again. Let's see what we can learn from it today."

"But I've told the story so many times I'm beginning to believe it's true."

"It is true, Mother. Dreams are true."

"But the story is always the same. Why go back to it again?"

"Because we're not, Mother. We're never the same."

And so she tells the story again, this time trying to recall the sense of rightness she felt when she let the angel walk away. She wants to hold that rightness again, now, when she needs it more than ever.

When she finishes, she gets up from her chair and fills her cup. Dara watches her, thinking how many times she has imagined her mother falling backwards into the snow creating an angel and letting it go. Her mother's ability to create life where there was none and her strength to let it live or die on its own had always held her in awe. She had always believed that her mother had powers beyond the rest of the world. Watching her now, though, as she tells the story, Dara is struck by the way Madeline holds her cup with both hands to keep it still. The skin of her hands around the cup is the translucent skin of an old woman. It's a trick, Dara thinks, an illusion she creates through distraction and studied quickness, like the card tricks and the money she plucked from thin air when the children were small, done to entertain, not truths, not lies. The thin skin on her hand, the slight shake of her head just gives her the appearance of being old, the spots on her hand painted there for effect. Somewhere behind the curtain, Dara thinks, her younger mother waits to make a grand entrance.

"Do you remember the magic tricks I used to do for you and your brothers?" Madeline asks suddenly. "I saw a magician on TV the other night. He made London Bridge disappear."

"You mean the one that fell down?" Dara asks.

"The very one," Madeline replies, as if the question had been serious. "I tried to see the trick, how he did it. But I couldn't see anything. It made my magic look so small, so out of date."

"You could add pyrotechnics to your act," Dara says.

"No," Madeline shakes her head. "No, I've hung up my cape for good."

Dara feels a chill breeze, as if from an early winter, and looks for something else to say. "Tell me another story. Make up the language as you go along."

"No!" Madeline says, unexpectedly loud. "No more stories! We've had enough stories, you and I. We're on the brink, both of us. You know that. I know that. It's time . . . time for something else." Words fail her and she looks around the cabin as if she will find what she needs in the things around her. "I want − I don't know. I just need to fix something."

And then, because really in the end there isn't much else for them to do, they look at one another and start to laugh.

"Fix something?" Dara says, her left eyebrow raised quizzically. "You mean fix something like the rain gutter that's hanging loose on the north side of the cabin or fix something like cookies? Because if I have a vote in any of this I say cookies."

"Oh Daughter," Madeline says, wiping her eyes. "Whatever will we do?"

They find themselves then at the water's edge. The morning mist has settled in, become a thick fog. The two of them work silently in unison, filling the gas tank, arranging vests, untying the ropes.

"Here," Dara says. "Put this slicker on. The day doesn't seem to think it's summer anymore." Madeline smiles, thinking about the subtleties of difference. To see her daughter move toward the caretaker's role, to begin to look out for the small needs of her mother, touches her.

"Next thing I know you'll be telling me to sit up straight," Madeline says as she pulls the starter on the small boat and maneuvers the craft away from the dock.

Their laughter is warm in the silvery mist. The excitement of their quest makes them almost giddy, like two young heroes setting off for foreign lands. For a moment above them a watery sun appears, but is soon swallowed by the mist. They look at one another, testing the depth of the other's desire to seek the unknown. They remember in that moment that they have been cautious all their lives, played by the rules, become the women they were taught to be. The risks they had thought they were taking in life were nothing compared to this moment, this quest. Nothing, really, has prepared them to do what they had decided to do.

"Where to, O Captain, my captain?" Dara asks.

"Wilson's Bay, of course," Madeline answers and opens the throttle, scooting them across the open water.

Within seconds the shoreline has disappeared and a thick and silent mist surrounds them. They find themselves without need of external signposts, feel no fear, no hesitation. Time may have stopped, for they no longer are aware of it. They will travel deeper and deeper into the mists, until they see it at last. Its eerie shape will rise from the water before their small boat as if it too were in search of them. And when they find it, it will be theirs. No stories will be told about this moment. They will possess it, and it them.

A FUNNY STORY

Today, while she was out of the room, her father died. She had stepped out for a moment because her head ached, he was sleeping, and she hadn't seen the sky in more than forty-eight hours. She had meant to get a bottle of water from the vending machine in the basement of the hospital and some Advil or something from the little shop that sells candy, angels, drugs, and the like and then return to his room. But the store was locked up when she got to it. The hours were posted. Open 11 a.m. to 7 p.m. She reread the sign carefully and then checked her watch. She walked to the end of the hallway to where a window looked out onto an enclosed courtyard. She couldn't see much, but it was daylight so her watch couldn't be far wrong, if at all. She read the hours again and then put her hand up to her forehead and peered into the store. It was no bigger than a refrigerator so she didn't know what she expected to see as she peered through the glass, maybe just an explanation for the discrepancy between Open sign and Closed fact. She breathed in through her nose and considered the smell of pain.

Not thinking about what she should do next, she started walking toward the exit sign. As she stepped outdoors she turned her face in the exact movement her mother always made when she baked. Her way of turning her face to the opened oven door seemed at once a protection from and homage to the rush of heat coming at her. She turned her own face to the side as the July heat hit her and felt a twinge of the familiar loneliness. What is life like for children who never know their parents, she wondered? Who would she be without this grief she holds like a precious gem?

She fished her keys out of her purse and stood at the edge of the parking lot. She could go anywhere, she thought. She didn't have to go back in there. She could pretend she's somebody else. Somewhere else. But she was too tired to imagine another who or another where.

She got into her car anyway. On her dashboard in the metal clip that holds reminder notes and directions she saw the prescription slip her husband had given her two days ago.

"You've got enough on your mind," he had said. "I can pick this up myself."

"Don't be silly," she replied and pulled the slip from his breast pocket. "I go right past the drugstore on the way to the hospital." She put her arms around the barrel of his chest and hugged him gingerly. He moved slowly in response, favoring a hurting back. She leaned her face into his neck and inhaled the clean, musky scent of soap and aftershave.

"I'll be home tonight by the time you get off work," she said. "You can take these muscle relaxants and I'll take a glass or two of wine and we'll be our usual fun couple selves, lolling in front of the TV. Dad will be fine at the hospital alone."

But when she walked into her father's room the rancid smell of a bowel movement nearly gagged her. She found him lying on his side, pulling himself hard against the metal handrail. The rank liquid spread out on the sheets behind him. His eyes were pinched closed and she could see one tear gliding along the bridge of his nose. When she touched his hand he let one sob loose before giving in to anger.

"Goddamn it I rang the bell and I hollered and I hollered and nobody came. What the hell am I supposed to do?

They've got me strapped down like some kind of Franken-
stein. Tubes and wires and god knows what else 'til a fellow
can't move and then they won't come when you need them."
His anger erupted as big and strong as it had been when he
was a young man, but his body was frail, birdlike in this institution's bed.

He took her hand. "Get me the hell out of here, Kate," he
said. "Get. Me. Out."

"I can't do that Dad. You know that." She started pulling
the soiled sheets away from him. When his gown wouldn't
pull free she ripped it in half. She was pulling clean sheets
from a closet in the hall when his nurse came.

"Here," she said. "Let me do that." She let the nurse take
the linen from her arms and followed her back into her
father's room. Like all the nurses here, she wore running
shoes that squeaked on the shiny linoleum.

So she stayed with him. Two days, going on three. Sleeping some in the chair beside his bed or on the couch in the
lounge down the hall, the days and nights ran together into a
kind of hum. When her father woke they talked mostly of the
past, because the present was too frightening.

"You don't have to stay," he told her in his more lucid
moments. Because she loved him she said, "No, I don't have
to stay. I want to stay."

Mostly that was true. As the days and nights wore on she
couldn't imagine not being there. Sometimes when she slept
she dreamed it was she who was sick and her father who cared
for her. She dreamed she was little again and he was stroking
her feverish forehead, but when she awoke, her head pillowed
in her arms on the side of his bed, he was trying to wake her,
moaning for pain medicine hours before it was time.

She brushed her hair out of her eyes and began to stroke
his arm. "It's too soon, Daddy." She lay her hand against his
forehead and began to sing softly, songs he had taught her,
songs her mother used to sing. It wasn't much, but it was all
she could give.

And all the while, her husband's prescription waiting to be filled.

From the front seat of her car she looked up at the hospital, counting the floors up to the sixth and then four windows over from the end to see the room where her father lay sleeping. Then she turned on the car and drove to the drugstore.

It was probably the large display of condoms that reminded her to ask for a refill on her own prescription. "Oh, I also want to pick up birth control pills while I'm here," she said to the white-haired man behind the counter who had been waiting on her for the six or seven years she had been shopping here.

"Do you have a prescription?" he asked.

"It's a refill," she said. "I usually pick up three months at a time, but last month you only gave me one and I didn't notice it until I got home."

"Your phone number, please." And then, "It'll be a few minutes." This was as chatty as he ever got, so she turned and wandered up and down the aisles while she waited, picking up things she didn't know she needed. A birthday card for her neighbor, shampoo, a roll of mints, a book of crossword puzzles. At the end of each aisle she checked to see if a new bag had been added to the basket of prescriptions near the cash register.

Finally she brought her armload of necessities to the counter and told the cashier her name. The pharmacist looked up and called across to her.

"I can't refill your prescription on birth control until tomorrow or else your insurance won't cover it."

She should have said, okay, no problem, thanks, let it go. She didn't need the pills yet; she was just trying to save herself a trip. But she was still groggy from hospital time and instead she said, "Why?"

"I can't refill your prescription on birth control until tomorrow or else your insurance won't cover it."

"I know that, but why?"

"Because your insurance won't cover it." He said it a little slower this time. "Apparently you're trying to refill your prescription too soon."

She blinked.

"But I usually pick up three months at a time and they let me do that, but last month I got only one month's supply. I just want to pick up the other two months."

"So tomorrow you can come in and get another two month's supply."

"I don't get the reasoning here," she replied. She smiled because she didn't want him to think she was angry with him. She became suddenly conscious that she hadn't washed her hair in two days, and that her shirt, more wrinkled than fashionable, had a small coffee stain near the third button. "What difference does it make if I get three months at one time or buy them separately. I mean, it's not like they're protecting me from an overdose or themselves from giving out too many pills, is it?"

The white-haired pharmacist pulled a paper out of his printer and brought it over to her.

"Here." He showed her a circled line. "It says here I can't refill your prescription until tomorrow or else your insurance won't pay for it."

"I'm sorry," she said, fighting back the desire to sit down on the floor and start crying. Exhaustion seemed to settle on her chest, heavy as an X-ray apron. "I don't mean to argue with you. I just don't understand why."

He tapped his pen to the print out and walked back to his station. The cashier took her card, her shampoo and mints and crossword puzzle book and started scanning each item. "He can't refill it until tomorrow or else the insurance company won't pay for it," she said helpfully.

"I'm sorry," she said again. "It's just that I don't get the logic of this. I don't mean to argue with you. I know it's the insurance company and not you guys. I just don't get it."

The cashier smiled at her, her eyes shifting to the line forming behind her. "You can come back tomorrow and the insurance company will cover it. Isn't that right, Jack?"

Jack, the white-haired pharmacist, looked up. "That's right. Tomorrow you can come in and get your usual three-month supply. But I can't give you any today or the insurance won't cover it."

She smiled at him and at the cashier as if she had finally gotten it and backed away. "Thank you," she said. "Thank you both. I'm sorry. I didn't mean to bother you."

In the car on the way back to the hospital she started laughing. Dad will get a kick out of this she thought. They both had a fine-tuned sense of outrage when it came to corporate absurdities. Once, years ago, when her Dad was trying to straighten out a problem on his telephone bill an exasperated clerk had said to him, "There's no reason for it. It's just our policy." That had become a standing joke between them. He had even used the line on her a few times when he didn't want to explain why she couldn't go somewhere or do something he didn't want her to do. "No, you can't go to a movie with that hippie," he would say. "I have no reason. It's just my policy." By the time she got back to the hospital she had turned the scene at the pharmacy into a funny story. Something that would remind them both of another life and time outside these walls.

One thing she had always liked about hospitals was the painted lines in hallways. Follow the blue line and you'll end up in the cafeteria. The red line will take you to the cardiac unit, the green to intensive care, pastel, of course, to pediatrics. They always seemed like little lifelines for the emotionally impaired, those confused by the current tragedy that had brought them to the institution. The single line past her father's room was brown; all the others turn off before you get to his hallway. She looked up when she got to that point where only a single line continued down the hall and it was then that she saw the commotion outside her father's room. Four or five people in white coats stood outside looking in.

Through this small crowd a technician maneuvered a cart that held, she later realized, a portable defibrillator. The paddles lay face up on top. She felt the back of her neck turn icy and the coldness moved down her arms, her back and into her legs. She kept walking toward the room though she wanted to run. She moved through the white coats easily, as if they weren't there. None of them looked at her.

His sheets were on the floor, kicked under the bed. His gown had been pulled wide open and was bunched up under his arms. His chin pointed to the ceiling as if an invisible string pulled him up, up. She went to his side and pulled his gown down, tried to cover his nakedness, to undo this final indignity. Only then did a nurse recognize her.

"We tried to reach you. We paged and paged but you wouldn't come." She pointed up to the sound coming over the intercom. "They're still trying."

"Would the daughter of the patient in room 6425 please come to the nurse's station on Six North." No names to hang onto; if the nurse hadn't pointed it out she would have missed it even then. She turned to the IV machine and began disconnecting tubes. "I'm sorry," the nurse said.

She stroked her father's chest, traced the burn marks left by the defibrillator paddles, and didn't know at all what to do next. There were no lines in this hallway. She wanted to know why it had to happen while she was away, while he was alone. She wanted to know why it had to hurt so bad. She wanted just to know why.

"I have a funny story to tell you," she whispered. "It happened, just now, while I was out of the room." Holding his hand, she told the story. She hurried toward the familiar punch line, hoping it could provide, if not an answer, at least some small measure of solace.

GLOSSOLALIA

"There's nothing as beautiful as beautiful love."
                              –Old guy in Saddle Creek Bar

What to do with that, beautiful love? My mind's eye touches always on my children's faces, sees the child in my father's face, my mother's light. She glows somehow in a way my words cannot describe. I fail in my every attempt. Maybe that's what parents do for us. Teach us to fail, accept failure, try again.

What have I learned, what can I teach? That morning light is kindest to the young, but worth the trade off – clear skin for stories. That good posture helps prevent migraines. That chocolate is sometimes better than sex but too much can give you a stomachache; like coffee it is both your friend and your enemy. That my father is a man of contradictions, both in his life and in my perception. That my mother is not a saint but can look like one when you want to be loved whether you're two or two hundred, which is how old I feel so much of the time when I think about love, beautiful love, so much a fairy tale it cuts me to the quick.

Today I am thirty-nine, the age my father was when I was born. Thirty-nine. The age I am. The life I'm living that is my life.

◦◦◦

What I want to remember is this: the shape of the moon the night I first took the title of wife, how the light reflected from that craggy surface onto the road ahead as we sped away from the familiar terrain I once called home toward a future known and unknown. It's the same moon looking back at me now. The same moon the four of us, you, me, our children, gazed at just last week when this big blue ball we live on moved between the sun and moon and turned a harvest moon blood red and beautifully, eerily strange.

What I want to remember is the shape of it that night, riding in that borrowed car. I remember thinking I would never be happier. That if I died then it wouldn't matter because I could never move higher, feel more than I did sitting there in that car beside you, my husband. Oh how those words, those labels and titles create an other outside of the us we made.

I remember thinking that, thinking those thoughts about happiness, but I don't remember the shape of the moon. I think—irrationally, I know—that if I could call up the exact image of that moon, remember the way its light struck the hood of that car I could recall too, the feeling, the lightness of pure joy, of being in love. But that moon hides its face and I don't remember her at all, as if she didn't exist on that particular night.

What I do remember is this, the way the moon lit the coast of St. Martin outside the restaurant where we dined and drank expensive champagne nearly two decades later. I can see it now, as if the image hovers between me and this page where I write the memory, I can see the way the moonlight struck the surface of the ocean, moon image appearing and disappearing in the swell of the waves, the light turning the froth of the surf into an eerie necklace at the base of the rocky shore.

I remember standing on the sand, the moon to my right a soft eye, to my left the hotel's spotlight on the cliff glaring down on this moment. You stood back on the rocks, watching, waiting. I walked down to the water's edge and felt the wave spend itself at my feet, its last lick up onto the sand felt like champagne on my toes. You, in shadows, did you smile back at me when I turned to you, beckoned for you to come join me in the moonlight?

What I want to remember always is the feeling of our daughter's body on my lap, our warmth reflected back on one another, the sight of our son wrapped in his sleeping bag, his face shining upward, watching the moon be swallowed by the earth's shadow. A moment out of time, in time. I want to remember this, witness to the moon, I want to hold it all, not just the image, but the feeling, the warmth of the body heat of this small family we form, the cool of the night air, the sense of the universe when the moon became a ball before my eyes, not a disc, flat and subject to the whims of sunlight and earth movement, an entity unto itself.

I want to remember this about the moon, that she shone without the sun; she exists in shadow.

She picked a piece of lint from her husband's lapel, brushed the nap flat with the back of her hand. Like all her actions involving her husband, her movements were shy, furtive. After forty-two years he still made her feel like a bride. This is not necessarily a good thing. To be a bride is to be by definition, new, inexperienced. Her bride-like feelings stemmed less from romance than from a confusion of roles: wife/daughter, father/husband. She would never have said this, or even thought it. No, that has been left to me to articulate, to explain to this page and to myself.

Articulate. Before I even begin, I diverge from her. Articulate, a word she would never have used, or understood. A word I wouldn't use in her presence. So here, on this altar of what I had hoped to be a communion of our storytelling souls I find myself setting up the barrier of language. Holding myself away from her with the very gift she gave me.

❧

My mother tells me about her miscarriages. I drive while she talks. The first one came early in the morning, before my father had left for the fields but after he had headed for the barn. She stood in the doorway calling his name. Each time she called out the blood gushed from her. During the long ride to town, the blood seeped through her coat, the one she had just gotten back from the cleaners the day before, and soaked the blanket upon which she sat. She tells me a nun baptized the fist-sized mass that passed between her legs. She does not tell me about the pain. She doesn't mention the uterine cramps you know she had. She doesn't tell me if she cried.

Her last miscarriage she baptized herself. I'm driving in heavy traffic when she tells me this installment and I can't ask her for details. Don't tell her I said this, but I irreverently picture her praying over the toilet.

She tells me how my dad worried so about her. This I can't picture at all and no matter where we are I can't ask her for details. I can't ask her how she knows. She tells me stories about a man I don't know. I have a black and white photo of the two of them. My mother stands stiffly, shyly smiling at the camera while my father grins, peering at the camera from behind her. Looking over her shoulder, his tanned arms wrapped around her waist, he's a man I can't even imagine. There must be some trick to the photo. I study it for signs of tampering.

My mother tells me stories. Her voice fills our life together. My earliest memories are of the sound of her voice, creating us, creating her, creating me.

❧

After my mother's surgery

That you have cancer is not reason enough
for me to love you more, but,
as it turns out, that seems to be what's
happening. I didn't think it possible
given how intensely I have loved you
and how long. I've hated you too sometimes
although guilt quickly put an end to that.
But anyway, that's all in the past,
today I am swabbing wounds that crisscross
a face too much like my own seen in a trick
mirror. Me in the future looking back
at the Me in the now. That you love me
is not in question here and I don't know why
I even think about it. What is in question
is how we're going to say goodbye when
the time comes. Because it will. Neither
your faith nor my lack of it will change that.

Notes on the death of a friend:

I'm at the stage of grief when I see you everywhere,
Richard, on the street, in a car next to me at the light, at a
restaurant table too far away to catch your eye. Always you
are turning away, out of reach, gone before I can call you.

I've lived long enough now to be able to say that, to say,
I'm in a stage of grief, to recognize what psychologists
describe, label, categorize, depersonalize. I am not unique in
missing you, a fact that only adds to my sadness.

I think I've reached the point where I can admit I'm angry
with you. I thought we were friends. You could have told me
you were dying. You had time. You could have let me know,
let me say goodbye. You dragged me into an intimate rela-

tionship with you – nothing physical or sexual, just an intimate meeting of fellow writers. I know things about you I shouldn't, not for the casual acquaintance this information I hold about your life. If you could write that stuff, let me read it, you could have told me you were dying. You could have let me say something to you. I don't know what, just something. Now here I am beneath these gray clouds with no place for this grief.

Oh hell, maybe it's not you I'm mad at. Maybe it's just the idea of being so alone in life, in the crowd of the living. Maybe I'm not mad at all. Maybe I'm just following the path, the stages of grief: disbelief, sadness, anger, bargaining, and finally acceptance. Maybe I'm just practicing for real loss. Is that what I'm supposed to learn here? How to negotiate the coral reef of loss? I like to think I'm supposed to learn something from every moment. It gives me solace to think there's a plan, that if I just pay close enough attention to the details I'll see the Big Picture. It's that side of me that longs to create a religion to replace the one that didn't take as a child. I don't know really, if there is a Big Picture. Maybe all is chaos. The butterfly beats its wings in Argentina and soon there's a thunderstorm in North America. All related, but all perched precariously on the smallest connections. No reason, just results. This follows this, but it might just as easily have followed that.

Chaos. And I'm looking for order, for consolation. What stage of grief encompasses the chaos? Does it make any sense at all? If it does, I can't see it. I'm stuck here in this Now, under this gray sky, missing you.

❧

My son again, this time wrapped in a blanket and my arms. The tornado warning siren whistling over the sound of wind and rain outside our window. Close to my ear he whispers, "I hope when I wake up tomorrow I can find myself."

❧

March 12, 1997. Today my students followed me from Andrews to Morrill Hall, trusting as cows. It's a safe assumption on their part that I wouldn't lead them to slaughter. Still, I felt nervous, worried for them, for me, for the whole precarious universe we live in. I counted three bicycles in the rack near the front door, noted that only the center stairs were cleaned free of snow, but I forgot to count the number of steps. Richard would have been disappointed in me. "Collect it all, Kate, that way when you sit down to write you can throw away the garbage and have gems to work with."

Inside the doors the two guys at the desk looked up expectantly when we walked in, not sure what to do when all eighteen of us walked past the donation box without even a glance in that direction. I thought about telling them I had called ahead, but didn't want to waste time.

Time, what the hell is that when you're standing in a building like Morrill Hall? I stood outside the case where the ancestors of the modern day elephants are shown in a series of pictures, each with a circle and a bar superimposed over it. Beneath is a sign, "Extinction is forever."

Then I went to the tree stump. I first saw it some thirty years ago, a girl scout away from home, all the way to Lincoln. Big trip, I thought, until I got to the space room. So small we are it's impossible to comprehend. The video of the moon's surface made me want to cry, not sure why. The beauty of the moon with the earth's eye gazing over its shoulder, the astronaut's voice describing his experience of feeling love, of feeling at home there on that barren surface. I wanted to stay there, listening and watching, but duty called, students waited, so I walked away.

What is it I want to take away from this? What do I want to remember? The sound of the rock wren or hawk? The feeling of peace that came with the first inkling of perspective? Why do I record this here now for some future self to come back to? What detail am I leaving out that, if recorded, would bring it all back, complete and real?

One student said trying to get all the students back into the classroom would be like herding cats. That's what it feels like now, trying to usher the collage of images into words to put down on this page, to chop pictures into thoughts.

The moon walk video has stayed with me. I can't stop thinking about the masculine, scientific voice saying he "felt a presence" on the moon. Maybe it was love. Maybe it was the collective energy of all those souls on earth watching them. Whatever it was, he didn't try to push it away. He didn't try to deny it. I wonder though if he didn't imagine it – the Doubting Thomas in me wanting to touch the wound, taste the blood. Why? Why do I doubt when I want so badly to believe in something outside of myself, larger than anything I know? Am I more afraid of being wrong than I am of being alone? My life is a process of seeking something to replace the religion of my childhood and yet when I'm confronted with evidence of something to believe in I question it, push it away. Richard seems to have gone to his grave at peace with his belief in no god. How did he do that? Why, before he reached that point in his illness where long talks were impossible, didn't he tell me something? Why didn't he at least point out the trail he took?

Because we all have to find our own way. Such an obvious, unsatisfactory answer. I don't see him on the street anymore. I no longer find myself stopping short, thinking I've caught a glimpse of him. Now I see people who remind me of him, have some trait in common with him – his eyes, his walk, his laugh. But even as I note it, I note his absence rather than his presence. This must be the acceptance stage. The one we the living work toward in our efforts to get away from the pain. Acceptance brings a kind of forgetfulness, doesn't it? And that's what makes it so hard. We want it, but we don't, because to begin to accept is to begin to forget. The lost become irrevocably lost. The dead irretrievably dead. Extinction is forever.

Oh, the lonely walk through Morrill is in me now.

And you find yourself praying. Letting go with something like emotion into the vast darkness of the night sky. You imagine your voice traveling into the sky to some other world. You think about ET phoning home. Corny stuff, but then you remember that in the end someone came for him. Somebody made him up, and then somebody took him home.

WITNESS
By Pam Barger

I push through one more overhead press,
though she stops mid-twist on the abdominals,
eyes a little wild, mouth turned up.
I've told her, since she insisted, I'm *Buddhist,*

an answer possibly easier to defend than
aggressively spiritual loner atheist-agnostic.
She wants to know what Buddhists think of Jesus.
She wants to know what I think will happen when I die.

I haven't a clue, I answer truthfully,
not having been dead yet, that I know of.
Which flips her to page twelve of the witness manual,
and she looks at me, all sympathy, saying,

That must be scary for you.
Not really, I lie, and ask about her new grandson
while I write *nine* on my Nautilus chart
and switch to the lateral raise machine.

I'm sad, because I always kind of liked this woman,
and I'm thinking about what I really want to say, which is,

of course I'm scared. I'm always scared.
I live scared.

What will happen when I die?
What will happen in five minutes?
I could run over a dog on my way home.
Iraq could bomb Omaha.

What if my daughter hates me,
my friends find out I'm selfish?
What if I freeze in hell for
skipping all those years of Mass?

I could witness to you, Phyllis.
I could suggest you're kidding yourself.
You believe that what you wish
is what will happen.

What if you return as a worm, Phyllis?
Or what if you just float off
like bubbles to the surface of water
boiling slow,

while your once-fit body shrinks
in that box with the cross on top,
turning, turning to hair,
bones, and dust.

Nebraska Novembers are somber months, not given to
spontaneity. The former prairies lie wet and sullen beneath
gray, sodden skies. According to the paper, assaults and sui-
cides start to go up around the middle of the month, the num-
bers making a steady climb toward the holidays. We are not
proud of these statistics, but we're a practical lot, here in our
square state in the middle of the nation. The sun will shine

again, we tell ourselves and each other. There are better days ahead.

It is at this point that my sister would remind me that ours is less a square state than a rectangular one. She being as literal minded as any high school geometry teacher finds herself incapable of letting such a detail slide without comment.

But of course, Mara, I would say, we're not literally a square. It was a figure of speech, a trope you might say.

No, she would inevitably reply. You might say. (Emphasis on *you* laden with meaning.) I would never call anything a trope. After all I didn't attend your big university. Trope or tripe, Nebraska is more a rectangle, not a square.

Thinking I might score a hit, I would say. Well, to the rest of the world, Nebraska is decidedly square.

Ah, yes, she would say with that slight lifting of her eyebrows that always signals the end of communication, then square we are.

Oh, for God's sake Mara, the point I'm trying to make has nothing to do with squares or rectangles, it's . . .

Did I hear you say for God's sake? But I had been given to believe that you and your friends had declared God dead.

Mara, I would say in total frustration, I am not now nor have I ever been a friend with Nietzsche.

It is at this point in the conversation that the balloon collapses. I'm not really talking to Mara at all. She's not here. She doesn't even exist except as a collaboration of my own perceptions. This is whole-cloth fabrication. It's what I do. When I'm anticipating a trip home, I start having conversations with different family members in the guise of fictional characters – it's easier that way. I think of it as lifting weights, something you do to gain strength.

The thing is, I never know when the fabric of civility that covers all our communication is going to rip, and conversations such as this, inane as well as mean, with none of us at our best, will suddenly become a reality. I say I fear them, but a part of me wishes for them. What would happen if we opened up and let one another inside?

❧

When my mother called us, she went through the names of all her daughters before she hit upon the one she wanted. I mostly answered to NancyMaryBrendaAnneKATIE, although sometimes she threw in an Irene or an Agnes, those being her sisters. Other times, in complete frustration, her own name tripped across her tongue. I grew up thinking it was a quirk, meaningless, hurry-made slips in sound only. Underneath the garbled syllables she knew me. But now memory makes new meaning, her calls become questions, her children become childhood repeated under new names. In her remembered gaze I see her confusion, her desire to know, where does self leave off and other begin?

❧

My mother has told me few stories about what I was like as a child. I was the sixth of seven children, what she remembers gets mixed up with my siblings. One story is of a time when I was about a year old. We lived on the south side of town in the house with the turret. Dad worked construction and was gone during the week. According to the story, I would get terribly sick during the week, high fever, lethargic, and Mom would worry and take me to the doctor who would find nothing wrong with me. On the weekend when Dad came home I would be well, my "old self." Dad would think Mom worried too much, that I was fine, out of the woods as my mother would say. Then Dad would leave for work on Monday and I would get sick again. I don't know how long this went on before they figured out the pattern. The solution: Dad started calling home on Wednesday nights just to talk to me. Me, a baby who couldn't talk back, but could only listen to a voice I must have thought had left me forever each time he drove away. The miracle of resurrection coming to me across the telephone lines. How Dad must have loved that, being so loved by a baby his absence made her sick. How much he must have loved me to squander the money – so precious then – on a phone call to a baby that couldn't talk.

✎

"Don't think even for a moment that you're not going to die."   –Dzongsar Khysenste Rinpoche

✎

The closest I've ever felt to god or nature? What comes to mind isn't the closest, but one of the farthest.

I was a sophomore and on my first religious retreat, at a convent in Norfolk with several other girls from St. Mary's. Ann, Pat, Jean, Cindy. Their young faces float up out of the collection of images that come to mind as I write. We were put into groups when we first got to the convent so that we were separated from our friends.

The first night we assembled in this large room and listened to speech after speech about what was ahead. The clock behind the podium was covered, as were all the clocks in the convent. They made us give up our watches, too. "When you walked in those doors you went on God's time," they told us. Then they made us stay up late, very late. Many of us fell asleep at the table. The next morning they got us up before the sun came up. They broke down our resistance through exhaustion. I didn't know it then but it's the same theory used in torture interrogations.

Through a series of goofy exercises our groups "bonded" and we became "best friends" with former strangers – not one of whom I can recall a single detail of today.

After forty-eight hours of bonding, we had "chapel hour." Each group would go into the chapel to pray together in the dark. We sat on the floor in a circle around a single candle and prayed together. We welcomed Jesus into our hearts and our lives. When we felt his presence we were to take the candle and testify our love to him. My group members cried and prayed and cried and prayed. One by one they took the candle and held it in one hand, wiping away tears of happiness with the other or holding the hand of a loving supportive group member. Finally everyone had testified except me. We cried together and we prayed together and they all focused the power of their love on my needs, my salvation. I felt nothing. Nothing but embarrassment and fear. We prayed some more. We cried some more. I couldn't feel his presence. I was a hollow shell filled only with myself.

"What's wrong, Katie? Why can't you let Him in?"

So I did. I took the candle. I testified to God's love and we all left. I walked out of the chapel into the waiting arms of my best friend. Pat cried with me, murmuring, "I know, Katie, it's scary." I thought she understood so I blubbered away on her shoulder. Then she said, "God's love is so wonderful it makes me cry too."

I felt the chill of a loneliness I had never known before.

When I heard my sister's voice, I knew something was wrong.

"Katie? I have bad news," she said. "Dad had a heart attack."

I don't know how long it took me to answer her. I remember the first thought was, Oh Daddy. I hadn't called him Daddy since I was a little girl, but at that moment that is who I saw, that tall strong man who was my Daddy.

I knew Brenda was struggling not to cry so I fought to keep my voice calm. "How bad?" I asked.

"I don't think he was alive when they took him out of here." That was all she could say. I told her I would be home as soon as I could. I would find Anne and we would all be there soon. "Don't worry," I said. "Everything will be all right." I didn't believe it. I just had to hear the words.

I turned to my boss and tried to tell her, but all I could say was, "Dad's had a heart attack. They don't think he's alive." I couldn't say the word dead.

On the way home my hands clutched the steering wheel so tightly I was afraid that I would suddenly develop the strength to rip it off the column. I concentrated on loosening my grip, then I went over the list of actions I had learned in drivers' ed: check road ahead, look in rear view mirror, check speed. I clung to those actions as a way of maintaining control of my emotions. I couldn't break down. I had to drive thirty miles home, find my sister and drive 200 miles to my parent's home.

I tried to pray but I didn't know what to pray for. I knew this had to happen. I knew if he were alive now we would have to do this again. And then there would be my mother. And then, on that drive, I touched in memory the faces of all those I loved and thought of all I had to lose.

⁓

Dear God,

Hi, it's me, Katie. But of course you know that. This is hard. Writing to you, I mean. (Oops, I'm supposed to capitalize all the pronouns that refer to You, aren't I? Sorry. But You know that, too, don't You?) Anyway, I've forgotten how to do this, addressing God, I mean. Once in a composition class I did one of the suggested genre exercises that included writing a prayer. I remember coming up with something, but don't recall at all what I said. I remember sitting in Dad's hospital room trying to pray. I remember driving from Seward to Lincoln not knowing if he were dead or alive, my mantra, "Oh please God, oh please God." Stopping now and again to pry, first one hand then the other from the steering wheel and reminding myself that this moment, this event, was part of the whole package. With life comes death and that praying for God to spare Dad's life was really only asking to delay the inevitable. I would then repeat to myself, "If not now then sometime." But always the chant would become, "please God, please God."

But now I'm talking about God, not to it. Try to imagine your audience for this letter, Katie, and start again.

The first images that come to mind are the trees and the river at Platte River State Park, the whole outdoors under an open sky, starry nights, blue skies at noon.

To the heavens I address these words:

But no words come.

To the sky I address this silence, this blank page filled with these squiggles of ink. I cannot render in words or thoughts any of this feeling that becomes prayer or communion with that which has no name. How presumptuous of humankind to believe in words as connection, in names as things.

⚬

Is this love?

Me pacing here. You lying there,
half in, half out of sleep.
Coming to only enough to tell me
about diarrhea, slow nurses, shitty sheets.
No tender moments here so I trim your nails,
blackened crescents under nails as hard
as horse's hooves.

The skin of your hand eerily soft,
as if even the ridges of your finger prints
have worn off. I hold each translucent finger
in turn. Clip yellow, jagged nails into smooth
half moons and wonder what it is, this thing
I do for you, this thing that needs doing.

No insights, just fragments of broken nails,
pieces of dirt, of dried blood littering

the bedspread stretched out beneath our hands.
I remember being told once that nails and hair
keep growing after death, that bodies dug up
appear to have been buried too soon. I think of that
as I struggle to tame the talon of your left
pointer finger. Out of the corner of my eye

I study the skeletal clarity of your face
upon this, another institution's pillow, and wonder
if it's true.

God you feel so lonely, and so pathetic in your loneliness.
This middle-class white girl angst is embarrassing, really. It
reminds you of your first broken heart. You were fourteen or
so. Your mother said, "Puppy love may not be real love, but
it can hurt just as bad." Your life is puppy love. You keep
looking for the real thing.

Today you are thirty-nine, the age your mother and father
were when you were born. Thirty-nine. The age you are. The
life you're living.